"All you have to do is stay away from us."

The warmth and humor disappeared from his face as he replied. "It's not that simple. You brought something into my life that I can't give up without a fight."

Diana looked at him aghast. She had no money to fight him in the courts. And there was no way she could win.

Her words were unsteady. "I suppose I am afraid . . . that you will take Noel away from me," she ventured, "and I will be left with—with nothing." She'd almost said "with neither of you."

"Look, if it will help, I'll introduce you to the best legal mind in London. I'll bet my last penny he'll tell you that, as the baby's mother, no one can take Noel from you."

Diana was shaken. He *did* mean to play fair—but he'd said "the baby's mother." Was that always going to trap her?

Marina Francis writes romance fiction because she knows from experience that great romantic love does happen. She and her scientist husband were engaged to be married exactly one week after they met and lived in unusual happiness until his sudden death years later. One of her earliest ambitions, to be a writer, was postponed for a successful singing career in North America and Europe. She began writing, usually to the accompaniment of music, after her husband's death, and says it gives her much comfort and satisfaction to bring about a happy ending to her fictional characters' problems. Her home is in Oakville, within sight of Lake Ontario.

Love's Perjury

Marina Francis

Harlequin Books

TORONTO • NEW YORK • LONDON
AMSTERDAM • PARIS • SYDNEY • HAMBURG
STOCKHOLM • ATHENS • TOKYO • MILAN

ISBN 0-373-02887-3

Harlequin Romance first edition February 1988

Printed in U.S.A.

CHAPTER ONE

DIANA REACHED the opulent jewelry boutique where she spent her working hours, breathless but on time. She knew that the Italian temperament that helped to make her boss one of London's top creative jewelers also made him impatient with minor irritations, such as apprentices who arrived late. But the autumn morning was so lovely that she had hurried across Hyde Park instead of crowding into the London Underground as usual. She had had to rush, but it had been worth it.

She paused outside the shop to see what Gian-Carlo had chosen to display. In this short street, filled with some of the most exclusive specialty shops in the world, she always felt that Gian-Carlo's shone out like a gem itself. As she gazed at the window display, Diana caught her breath with delight. There, gleaming against the lush depth of dark blue velvet, lay a magnificent set of jewelry: necklace, earrings, bracelet and pin, wrought in yellow gold and set with diamonds and deep pink coral. It was a fabulous example of the unusual combinations of gems for which her boss was famous.

"You like?" Gian-Carlo greeted her as she went into the boutique.

"I haven't the words," Diana said, shaking her head. "Gian-Carlo, you are a genius."

"*Si*," he agreed with matter-of-fact composure, but she could see he was pleased with her enthusiasm. Then he moved toward the stairs to his workshop, but he stopped suddenly. "Ah!" he exclaimed. "Nearly I forget." He turned and seized Diana's forearm with an operatic gesture. "There has been a man—" leaning toward her, he whispered conspiratorially "—for *you* he is asking."

"Me?" Diana looked closely at him. She was used to gathering more meaning from Gian-Carlo's expressive hands and eyebrows than from his words.

"*Si.* For sure he said Miss Verney." He gave her an interested smile. "Maybe you have the boyfriend, yes?"

"No—" Diana shook her head "—no boyfriend."

Gian-Carlo pursed his mouth and made an appreciative inspection—from her dark gold hair, down past her neat, high breasts to her long slender legs and then back to her waist and up again. His eyebrows and ear-high shrug said something between "What a waste!" and "Who are you kidding?"

Diana smiled. She knew Gian-Carlo was an incurable romantic, but in his case it was not a fault. His romanticism was part of the temperament that produced the ravishing jewelry that flattered every woman who wore it.

"Did this man say he would be back?" she asked.

"No, but he will be," Gian-Carlo assured her as he went up to his workroom.

Diana shrugged and settled herself at her small worktable at the back of the showroom. As she laid out her tools she idly went over in her mind the few men she knew in London. She was certain none of them had ever been to the shop. They had all been her sister Kris's friends. She remembered them as a nice crowd—lively, good-looking and clever. Just the types one would expect a top model like Kris to have around her. However, Diana hadn't seen much of them, for shortly after she had joined her sister in London, Kris had had to step out of the party-going scene.

Diana had gone with her to break the news of Kris's pregnancy to the head of the model agency she worked for.

"Pregnant!" the man had moaned. "The mind boggles. The very word makes me think of wet nappies and warm milk. A far cry from the Kris image of handmade lingerie and chilled champagne."

Kris had given him a kiss and her irrepressible giggle. "Never mind, darling. I won't be gone forever, you know."

Diana remembered the icy finger of apprehension that had traced her spine at her sister's words. She had shrugged it off and told herself that it was natural to feel a bit emotional at a time like that.

The agent had spoken disconsolately—"Well, let's keep it a secret as long as we can"—and Diana had had some sympathy for him, but she was sure that her warmhearted sister would make it up to him when she got back to work.

When she got back?

Who could have suspected that the baby who was to cut the agent's income for a while would rob the lovely Kris of so much more than money?

Diana forced her mind away from that memory and brought it back to her work. She was still vaguely wondering about Gian-Carlo's mysterious visitor, and then suddenly she had an answer. She remembered the stunning woman who had tried on a pair of earrings the day before. They were Diana's own design and one of the first Gian-Carlo had judged good enough to go in his showcase. She had been thrilled that such a sophisticated customer was interested in them.

"I love the way they come forward on the cheek," the woman had said, "but I think I would like them in gold instead of silver."

Diana's heart leapt. She knew they would be fabulous in the more precious metal, and her fingers itched to fashion them, but she knew, too, that gold would send the price sky-high. The design was large, even barbaric, but this chic woman could certainly "carry" it. Diana crossed her fingers for luck and called Gian-Carlo to give an estimate.

"Eighteen-karat gold, of course, madam?" he asked calmly.

"Naturally." The woman was just as calm. Then Gian-Carlo named a price that made Diana smother a gasp, but didn't turn a single hair on her customer's fashionably-coiffed head.

"Not at all unreasonable," the woman had said, "but just to keep peace in the family, perhaps I'd better have my husband see the earrings before I give you a firm order. I'll ask him to drop in tomorrow."

That was probably the mystery man, Diana decided. She felt sorry she had missed him, but if he was really interested he would be back.

The day passed as usual and Diana gave no more than a passing thought now and then to her early-morning caller, but she hoped the man would show up. She didn't have the chance to work in gold very often since mistakes could be costly, but this was her design, and she was sure that Gian-Carlo would let her make the earrings if the order came through.

Her musing was interrupted when a dark figure cast a shadow on the glass door of the shop. A man came in, and Diana's first impression was simply of size. Her eyes traced the broad shoulders that filled much of the doorway, and followed the line of his figure to a slim waist and long, muscular legs. His dark suit and quiet tie contrasted sharply with an immaculate white shirt and did their best to proclaim him a successful London businessman. Yet they did nothing to soften the impact of his masculinity, which was as potent as if he wore a buccaneer's kerchief and carried a cutlass in his belt.

"Miss Verney?" he asked as he came farther into the shop. They were on the same side of the counter and as he stepped toward her, Diana felt an unaccountable need to take refuge behind it. She told herself this was nonsense; she had met plenty of handsome men before. As the stranger crossed the floor, she managed to hold her ground until he was close enough for her to see the shadow of a dark beard under the healthy skin of his cleft chin, and to smell the faint tang of expensive after-shave. He stood, quietly waiting for her answer with a controlled, intimidating stillness, while his gray eyes scanned her with cool scrutiny. She felt the pull of sheer animal magnetism tingle across her nerve ends. Was this what they called machismo? she wondered. He must surely be her customer's husband, for she had never seen *this* man before—she would have remembered him if she had.

"Yes, I am Diana Verney," she answered as she retreated behind the counter. "Your—your wife said you might be in."

"My wife?" A corner of the man's mouth lifted in a cynical twist. "You have mistaken me for someone else. My name is David Farnham. I am Jeremy's brother."

The light of the shop suddenly dimmed for Diana. The blood sang in her ears and her breath fought in her chest. With a real effort she managed to steady herself against the counter and forced herself to look with apparent composure into the darkly handsome face still watching her dispassionately. She fought down the panic brought on by the sound of a name that held for her only memories of loss and heartbreak.

As she met his eyes, so heavily fringed with black lashes, she remembered where she had seen such eyes before. They were exactly like his brother Jeremy's. But Jeremy could no longer harm her, and what could any other Farnham want with her after all these months? She told herself that her fear was unreasonable; nevertheless she was suddenly swamped with unanswered questions, confused memories and frightening speculations.

David Farnham was still looking at her with cold detachment. "Miss Verney, would it be possible for me to talk with you for a short time?"

Something within Diana wanted to shriek "No! No!" but common sense told her that if this man was bringing trouble she had better at least know what form it might take. It was possible that her panic was unnecessary, but she couldn't stop the alarm bells ringing in her head. She needed time to think...to weigh the situation. Then, with relief, she heard Gian-Carlo's footsteps on the stairs. His presence would give her an excuse to postpone any conversation.

"I'm sorry, but I can't talk here, Mr. Farnham," she said, her voice as steady as she could manage.

"I was afraid of that," he replied, "but I must talk to you on a matter of some importance. You had better telephone my secretary and arrange a time that will suit both of us."

"Very well," she nodded, and took the business card he offered. He gave her a brief nod, turned on his heel and left without another word.

Gian-Carlo's voice reached her ears. "So he *does* come," he said in an I-told-you-so tone. "And he goes so soon?"

"It wasn't a business matter," Diana said, and she could sense Gian-Carlo's struggle between approval at her dismissing a personal visitor so quickly, and disappointment at not seeing more of her "romance."

For Diana, all the light had gone out of the lovely morning. She couldn't remember Kris ever mentioning a David Farnham. All her talk had been about the brother, Jeremy,

the father of her expected child. Since her sister's death a
recurring fear had haunted Diana—the fear that one day a
Farnham might appear, to try to claim the beautiful little
baby boy who couldn't have been more dear to her had he
been her own child. And now, perhaps, it had happened.

If only she had done the right things sooner!

For months she had been telling herself that it was time
she took steps to make herself Noel's guardian by law as well
as by circumstance. She had no idea how such things were
done, but she had felt that she should wait until she had
more to offer. She had thought it was hardly likely that the
authorities would officially hand over a baby to a young
woman with no husband, no suitable home and no job. She
had decided to leave well enough alone until there was time
for her to build up a backlog of security.

On the night she had taken on this heartbreaking responsibility, she had known that it wouldn't be easy, but she had
accepted it willingly. Her sister's life was hanging on a
thread as the baby lay in his mother's arms for the first—
and last—time. Like most babies born by cesarean section,
he was quite perfect, unmarked by the trials of normal birth.
Diana had gazed down with awe at the small flawless face,
the tiny helpless hands, the delicate petal-fine skin. Then
Kris had whispered, with her last flicker of strength, "Will
you take him, Diana? Please! Please tell him how much I
wanted him...and, oh, promise that you'll love him...just
love him...."

For the last time Diana had looked into her sister's velvet-brown eyes, and felt her heart break as she gave her
promise.

Her sister had died that night. Diana, the next of kin, had
taken the baby, but she had known that the father, if he
wanted to, could probably make a strong case for the cus-

tody of his son, especially if he could afford a top-rank
lawyer to argue for him.

Diana groaned. Why, oh why hadn't she pressed for legal guardianship sooner?

She hadn't had much except love to give the little boy in
the past months, but he had never gone short of that. At
first he had been an outlet for all the pent-up affection the
loss of her sister had stored within her. But then, after a few
weeks, he was no longer just something to fill her arms,
something to cuddle and croon over. Almost overnight it
seemed, he'd become a little person who smiled at the sound
of her voice, who grasped joyously at her face and hair, who
did his best to tell her that he was glad to see her when she
bent over his playpen. With every day he became more precious. She couldn't imagine life without him. No, he never
had been without love, and he never would be as long as
she—As long as what? She couldn't finish the thought with
the menacing figure of David Farnham towering in the back
of her consciousness.

Diana was suddenly thrust into the present by the arrival
of her customer of yesterday, complete with an obviously
indulgent husband. But even the satisfaction of getting the
order for the gold earrings did little to lift her anxiety.

Gian-Carlo seemed to sense that she wasn't herself, and
told her, "Go home, *cara*. It is Friday, God be thanked.
This trouble that bothers you will be gone by Monday,
yes?"

Diana was thankful to go, but she knew that her trouble
would not be over by Monday, or any other day, until she
had spoken with Farnham, until she knew exactly what he
wanted from her. In which case, the sooner she met with him
the better.

She turned back to the shop and, locating the business
card in her purse, picked up the telephone. So, he's chair-

man of the company, she noted as she dialed. A politely disinterested voice answered, "Farnham Industries. May I help you?"

Diana very nearly hung up, but she knew she must go on. There was no way she could avoid David Farnham forever. She would have to talk to him sooner or later, this man who bore exactly the same relationship to the baby as she did...and who had infinitely more power to protect that relationship than she had.

"May I help you?" The words were repeated with slightly annoyed insistence.

"Mr. David Farnham, please. My name is Diana Verney."

"One moment, please." The line was switched at once.

"Oh, Miss Verney, thank you for calling." This second voice was definitely top-quality secretary material, Diana thought. "Mr. Farnham told me to expect your call. When will it be convenient for you to see him?"

Diana wanted desperately to answer "Never!" but a more sensible inner voice warned her to keep her head. She knew her fear of David Farnham was as yet without a solid base. It was purely instinctive, and her safest course would be to find out as soon as possible what he had in mind. All she was sure of was that it was bound to affect Noel.

The secretary was continuing. "Mr. Farnham is tied up for the rest of the day, I'm afraid, but he did suggest that you have lunch with him tomorrow at the Hilton."

Humph! Diana sniffed to herself. Just the type to expect her to be impressed. Well, she had no intention of being intimidated by a luxury hotel. She thought quickly. Two things were important: she wanted to spend as little time as possible with Farnham, and she wanted to meet him in a public place.

"No, I can't do that," she answered curtly, "but I'll have tea with him in the Carbury tomorrow at four."

That was clever, Diana congratulated herself as she hung up. The eminently respectable Carbury was within easy walking distance of her place, and people weren't expected to linger too long over afternoon tea.

Nevertheless, as she stood up, Diana was sorry that she had been so abrupt. After all, the secretary had only been doing her job. It was when she found herself doing short-tempered things like that, things that were out of character, that she realized how the strain of the past year had worn her down.

Possibly too, that was the reason why this man's visit had so unnerved her. He had said very little. Why should she take it for granted that David Farnham would upset her life? Quite likely she was reading far too much into his appearance on the scene and— She stopped short with a gasp. While she had been dawdling, Mrs. Larkin, her landlady, would be waiting for her to collect Noel.

Diana hurried home and turned to her landlady's ground floor apartment. As usual, as soon as she stepped into the cozy sitting room she felt better. A brisk fire crackled in the grate and a puffed-up canary trilled in a cage in the window alcove. What a wonderful piece of luck it had been, she thought for the hundredth time, to find someone like Mrs. Larkin to look after Noel when she was at work. He was a sweet-tempered baby, but still, Diana knew there weren't many capable women these days who were willing to look after a lively, nine-month-old boy, no matter how much they were paid.

"Come in, luv, come in and warm yourself." Diana felt better just at the sound of Mrs. Larkin's voice. It was as comfortable as her figure. "That east wind fair cuts you in two, doesn't it?" Diana agreed that the London weather had done its usual about-face, and that a delightful morning had changed into a bitter evening.

That sent her mind back once more to her meeting with David Farnham. "Mrs. Larkin," she said, "do you think you could possibly look after Noel for an hour or two tomorrow afternoon? I have a business appointment that I simply can't get out of. I know you like to keep your weekends free, but it would be a big help if you could manage it just this once."

"Yes, I think I could, luv," the landlady said, nodding. "I am only going over to my sister's, and I could take him with me. He's no bother, but I might not be back until after six. Would that be too late for you?"

"No, just fine." Diana felt instant relief. "Thank you, Mrs. Larkin," she said. "I don't know what we would do without you." And that was no lie, she thought, carrying the baby upstairs to her own apartment.

Noel was in his usual high spirits, slapping at her cheeks with enthusiasm to let her know that he was glad—no, absolutely delighted—that she was back. Diana ducked as a wet, wholehearted kiss found her chin. "Now, look here, young man, passes like that leave me cold," she told him. Noel beamed at her in total disbelief and gurgled as she returned the kiss with a noisy smack.

She bathed him and fed him and tucked him into his cot. He always fell asleep quickly, like a happy puppy, and Diana looked down at him with deep love and compassion. Poor little fellow! Life had taken a couple of nasty swipes at him already. She would stand between him and as many other blows as she could, she promised, but she shivered as her mind jumped ahead once more to the next day's appointment with David Farnham.

With annoyance Diana told herself to think about something else. Already her mind seemed to be going around in circles, and she knew it would be better to save her energy until she had a definite problem to solve. She went to her small kitchen to see if food would help her forget, even temporarily, the ordeal she would have to face.

But when she looked at the food she had put out, she smiled. Funny how one went back to childhood things for comfort, she thought. A mug of hot chocolate and a plate of peanut-butter sandwiches had been the favorite cure-all for Kris and her whenever life became too much for them, which it had fairly often after their parents were divorced.

Diana had been five years old and Kris barely ten when their mother had finally decided that she'd had enough of the gray streets of Oxford. Its "dreaming spires" might draw their millions of admirers, but for her the yachts of the south of France and the tables of Monte Carlo were infinitely more attractive. The outstanding beauty, which she had passed on to Kris, had been her passport to that world, and she had left her daughters with only the memory of an enchanting person who had looked beautiful, felt soft and silken, smelled delicious—and had deserted them.

They hadn't missed her too much at first, though, as they were used to being left with a nursemaid, but when it finally sank in that she was never coming back, the two sisters were bereft and lonely. It was then that Diana had clung to Kris, her one solace, and Kris had always been there to cuddle her and hush her to sleep.

Their father had cloistered himself in the university where he headed the history department. He would have been utterly astonished if anyone had suggested that his daughters, of whom he had reluctant custody, needed anything more than a well-furnished house and an extremely competent housekeeper.

The little girls had grown close through the years and shared all their hopes and small triumphs. Then, when Kris

had decided to become a model, Diana had been caught up
in her sister's excitement, and the two of them had giggled
delightedly for hours over such a thrilling prospect.

"Mind you, I'll have to change my name," Kris had said.
"Cressida! Imagine! It's impossible!"

Diana had had to admit that it wasn't too good. Profes-
sor Verney had been immersed in ancient Greek history
when his first daughter had been born and had named her
accordingly. Diana was often thankful that he had pro-
gressed to the Romans before she had come along, and she
had got off lightly with the name of the goddess of the
moon.

"Cressida...Cress...Crass...Cross..." her sister had
mumbled on. "It wouldn't be so bad," she said, "if people
didn't always shorten my name to Cress. I'm tired of
sounding like something to put on a sandwich. Where's the
glamour in that? Cressy...Crissy..." she went on.
"Cristy...Cris... That's it! Kris! With a *K*. It doesn't sound
all that different from Cress but it has a lot more oomph.
How about that, then?"

"You don't think it sounds too masculine?"

"Not a bit. That will just be an extra gimmick for me. It
will help to keep my name in people's minds. Add a dash of
spice."

"I thought you wanted to get away from edibles." Diana
giggled, and ducked Kris's playful slap. At least, she had
thought, looking at Kris's slender curves, no one would ever
forget her sister was a woman once they had seen her.

It had all been just good fun until Kris left for London.
Diana remembered her own desolation, but she had been
comforted by Kris's promise that she would send for her just
as soon as she could.

"Cheer up, Diana. I just know things are going to work out for me, and then you can catch the first train. It will be absolutely wonderful. We'll have a ball!"

Naturally Diana had fully expected her sister to be an immediate success, but looking back on it now she realized it had been the sort of story that was usually too good to be true. Kris's rare combination of silver-gilt hair and eyes like brown velvet pansies had grabbed the attention of the fashion world, and when that lofty world found that she also had a warmhearted generosity and a joyous sense of fun that came through in her photographs, her popularity zoomed. In a year the name Kris was known to every top photographer in London.

Diana remembered, too, Kris's delight when Diana had told her about her scholarship to a notable college of art in Scotland.

"Good for you!" Kris had exclaimed. "I always knew you were the brainy one." And when Diana found that her real flair was in jewelry design, Kris was ecstatic. "What could be better? London is the best place in the whole wide world for that sort of thing, and who better to show it off than 'the fabulous, enchanting, intriguing, beautiful'—and so on, and so on—'Kris'?"

Diana laughed. "You've been reading your own publicity," she teased. Nevertheless she knew that all those wonderful adjectives really did suit her sister.

"I shall absolutely refuse," Kris had gone on, "to wear any jewelry but yours in my photographs."

When another two years had passed and the end of her course was almost in sight, Diana began to count the weeks to the time when she would join her sister. It would be exciting and glamorous and stimulating.

But when Kris's letter had come, it hadn't been about splendid parties, fashionable gowns and exotic foreign places. It had simply said, "Can you come to me now, Diana? Please! Please! I need you very much."

There had been no explanation, just the heart-touching appeal. Diana had rushed to London to find her lovely sister still devastatingly beautiful, still glamorous, still sought-after—and pregnant.

With her usual lightheartedness, Kris had tried to make the best of the situation, but Diana knew she must be worried or she would never have sent that urgent call for help. And that was when Diana had first heard the name Farnham.

"Jeremy Farnham and I have been, er, close friends for a long time," Kris had explained, "but we hadn't planned on getting married or anything like that."

Diana hadn't been really surprised. For a long time she had known Kris's attitude toward taking a lover without a long-term commitment, but she also remembered the reason for it. Kris had been the real victim of their parents' broken marriage; the one who had been left without the love and affection that most ten-year-olds take for granted. She might easily have turned into a selfish little monster, but instead she had poured out all her inborn warmth to her small sister. Certainly Diana had loved Kris in return, but at five she had been far too young to do more than cling to her sister. When Kris had needed it, she had never known the support of caring parents or older siblings. No wonder she had avoided making a long-term commitment to anyone, when in her heart she had doubted that such a thing really existed for her.

And now here she was, once again waiting for someone she believed in to come back and support her through the greatest emotional and physical trial of a woman's life. But where was this man—this Jeremy Farnham—when Kris needed him so badly?

"Honestly, Diana," Kris had tried to reassure her. "Jeremy won't let me down. It's just bad luck that he's away. Something to do with the Near East or the Far East—oil, or something like that. He phoned me in a terrific rush just before he caught a plane. A business flap was on, and he had to leave at once."

"And you didn't tell him about the baby?"

"My dear, how could I? I didn't know then."

"Well, can't you write to him? It might get him back here sooner," Diana urged. For some reason that she couldn't explain even to herself, she felt uneasy that the baby's father wasn't standing by.

"No, I'll just have to wait for him," Kris explained. "When I asked for his address, his office told me that his mail was being held until he got back. Anyway—" her inimitable giggle was back for a couple of seconds "—I want to see his face when I tell him. I wouldn't miss it for the world! And, believe me, there'll be champagne and roses. That's Jeremy's style. Just wait until he knows I need him. You'll see."

As time went on Diana saw Kris becoming more and more wrapped up in the coming of her child. On the surface she was just as fun loving as ever, but her whole life gradually became geared to the baby's arrival. Yet Diana was still uneasy. If only Jeremy Farnham were here to give Kris whatever support she might need.

"Are you sure you *want* to marry Jeremy?" Diana asked her one day. "You always used to say that you liked running your own life and could get along just fine without a husband. And goodness knows, with the money you earn you could easily support a child." Diana didn't want to see her sister forced into a situation that might bring her more grief in the long run.

"I know I used to say that," Kris answered, "but it's funny how expecting a baby changes the way you think. I seem to have a whole new outlook on things. I just want the very best for my baby and that includes having a father. I want my baby to have a name." She had gone on, "Jeremy doesn't have to *stay* married to me if he doesn't want to." But when Diana heard the strain behind her sister's laugh, she realized how much Kris was counting on having a husband and a legitimate father for her child.

The weeks passed, and Diana's anxiety grew as she watched Kris become increasingly caught up in the idea of Jeremy's getting back before the birth. At last, in desperation, Diana telephoned his office but got little satisfaction. A polite secretary told her that Mr. Farnham was expected back probably some time in November, but the answer hadn't sounded at all definite. Nevertheless, when Diana confessed to Kris what she had done, her sister had sounded cheered.

"Good! Since the baby isn't expected until January, that will give Jeremy plenty of time to make an honest woman of me." Then she laughed. "Honestly, Diana, I think you are more worried about this whole business than I am. Jeremy *will* get here in time."

But Kris had been wrong.

Jeremy Farnham had been late. Much too late.

CHAPTER TWO

DIANA AWOKE to a dreary, dank and dismal Saturday, and she felt no real urge to brighten it. The only yearning she had was to pull the bed covers over her head and sink back into oblivion. But that was too much to hope for. Noel was already showing signs of restlessness, and David Farnham would surely show up for their appointment, whether she got up or not. She sat up abruptly. Probably if she plunged into her customary Saturday-morning routine, she would be able to forget the afternoon for a few hours.

She fed Noel and settled him in his playpen, and then did her weekly cleaning. When she had finished she looked around the apartment and wondered what a person like David Farnham would think of it. Not much, she suspected. It was a fairly typical "furnished accommodation," but it was the best she could afford at the moment.

The decor ran to cream walls with everything else in tired shades of green, but she would have put up with a lot worse for the sake of having the invaluable Mrs. Larkin for Noel. A few bright posters, several colorful cushions and a plant or two had been her only additions so far, but the future was beginning to look promising for her now. She knew she would be able to do more to the rooms very soon.

Things had been quite different when she had met David Farnham's brother, Jeremy. That meeting had been in her sister's place, another sort of apartment entirely. No two or three rooms in a colorless rooming house for Kris. It had been a luxurious suite in a typical London converted mansion, Victorian in its opulence.

"Isn't it gorgeous?" Kris had asked as she showed Diana around for the first time. "It's old-fashioned, of course, but marvelous for parties. Those big rooms and high ceilings... and thick walls," she added, giggling. "No elevators, granted, but the stairs are no bother."

That was true, they were no bother, but they had been Kris's death warrant.

Diana knew that the memory of those stairs would stay with her for the rest of her life.

On the morning of Christmas Eve, Kris, heavily pregnant, had stepped out of the apartment door to pick up the daily paper, and her eye had caught a paragraph heading: "Whirlwind Marriage of Sir Edwin Farnham's Younger Son to American Beauty." Diana could still hear the crash and see the pitiful heap of her sister's body at the foot of the stairs, far below.

The rest of that day had been a chaotic blur of speed and misery... the soul-sickening sound of the hurtling ambulance turning sharp corners—corners that were merry with bell-ringing Santas... the long white corridor of the hospital with its tinseled Christmas tree... the crisp efficiency of the emergency ward that suddenly had barred Diana from her sister's agony. Then came the long, long hours in the waiting room, hours that had ended with the start of a baby's life and the snuffing out of his mother's.

Diana remembered the multitude of problems that had fallen in on her at once. Kris had lived long enough to give the baby into her care and although Diana knew that she was hardly the ideal guardian for a small baby, she was determined to cope somehow, to keep the promise made to her sister, at any cost.

Shortage of money had been her biggest worry. Certainly Kris had made a lot, but she had spent it as quickly as it had come in. After all, it had been natural for her to expect years and years of a highly paid career ahead of her.

There had been frighteningly little money left in Diana's purse when she had opened Kris's door on a January morning to an elegantly blasé Jeremy Farnham. As she swung back the door, she knew at once who he was. He was exactly what she had expected: young, debonair, utterly sure of himself—and she wouldn't have trusted him as far as she could throw him. He might have made a perfect match for her lovely sister on a dance floor or in a fast car. But as a husband and father . . . ? Diana shuddered.

She took a deep breath to steady her nerves and watched his experienced eyes scan her from the top of her head to her ankles, the tip of his tongue skimming his lower lip all the while. For one awful, primeval moment she felt an urge to rake her fingernails down his smooth cheeks.

"Hello! I'm Jeremy Farnham . . . but I've never seen *you* before!"

"You'd better come in," Diana said, stepping back to avoid any contact with him.

"I've come to see Kris. Is she in?"

"No."

He lifted an eyebrow as he stepped through the door. "Well, that might not be such a devastating disappointment," he said with a knowing smile as his eyes roved over her figure once more.

"Sit down, please," she said, motioning him to a chair.

"After you." He bowed with a mocking flourish.

"Sit down!" Diana repeated with harsh emphasis. "This is no time to play the fool." She saw surprised resentment on his face as he moved toward a chair.

It didn't take long to tell her pitiful story, for Diana felt no need to spare this man's feelings. She saw him practically crumble, but she felt that his principal concern would be for his own skin, for what the story might do to him in his particular world. He made some display of grief and uttered the expected cry of "Oh, if I had only known!" but Diana couldn't bring herself to believe a word of it.

At last, when he had gone, she went into the bedroom and picked up the sleeping baby—the baby whom Jeremy Farnham hadn't even asked to see—and cradled him against her breast as she wept away her anger and her pain and her grief. She hoped she would never see that man again, but he had given her another reason for keeping the baby as her own. Jeremy Farnham was the last person in the world who should come near Noel.

Only one useful thing had come out of Jeremy Farnham's visit. He'd made it clear that he would pay for the baby's support. Diana felt that he was probably protecting himself from the publicity of any future claim, but she'd accepted the money for she needed it badly. Nevertheless, her relief at having her immediate financial worries removed was tempered by the thought that she wanted to keep as great a distance as possible between Noel and the Farnhams. The day would surely come when she would be able to support him without help from anyone, and when it did, she wanted Noel to be free of any other ties. For the present, however, she would accept for the baby's sake the help they so sorely needed.

For a few months Jeremy's cheques came regularly, and the money was very useful. Kris's elegant apartment had had to go, and it hadn't been easy, with a young baby, to find another place, but Diana had managed. Then came the terrible morning when she had turned on the radio news and heard about the disaster in the English Channel. There had been a sudden squall and several yachtsmen had been lost.

Jeremy Farnham had been one of them.

"What a waste" had been Diana's immediate reaction, his young face still fresh in her mind, but she hadn't fully realized at first just how much his death was going to mean to her, that suddenly there was no one to send money for Noel. Once again she was on her own.

Then had come the black time when she'd been close to the end of her tether, when she had pored over want ads, haunted employment offices, scoured mean streets, looking for a job—anything to keep Noel with her. Then at last, like the sun breaking through the clouds, she had found her new job and the apartment at Mrs. Larkin's, all in the same week.

Life was wonderful! Diana had a few months of being happy again, of once more feeling in control of her destiny... and Noel's, too.

And now David Farnham had walked into their lives.

It was useless to speculate on how he had found her, and particularly on what he might want of her. He must have heard about the baby. Diana had hoped that the high-fashion scene of her sister's world was far enough removed from the high-finance world of the Farnhams to make the discovery of Noel unlikely. And now what was she to be faced with? Well, she would know soon enough.

Her immediate problem was choosing the right thing to wear. No vanity was involved. Far from it! She simply wanted to look sensible and capable, capable of caring for a baby boy. Her plain navy blue suit with a simple white blouse would be about right, she thought. Dressed like that she could forget her appearance. There would be plenty of more important matters to concentrate on.

Diana brushed her shoulder-length hair until its dark gold gleamed and then pinned its curling ends to the top of her head. An unswept hairdo always made her feel taller than her five feet seven, a little more dignified and businesslike. She felt she was going to need every slight advantage she could find.

She gave herself a last scan in the mirror. She looked too pale, she thought. Anxiety had faded some of the color from her cheeks and lips, and she replaced it with a sparing brush of rouge and a fingertip of lip gloss. That would do, she decided, nodding. She didn't want to look either harassed or worried—or anxious to please, for that matter.

As she waited until it was time to leave, her worries of the night came crowding back. If Noel was the reason David Farnham wanted to meet with her, could he *really* take him from her? Would he want to if he could? Where could she turn for advice if she needed it? These thoughts had raced around tirelessly in her head for hours like squirrels in a cage.

She went to the window to have a look at the weather. Noel was already downstairs with Mrs. Larkin, and the sky was darkening. She hoped they wouldn't be caught in the coming shower. Thank goodness the Carbury was within walking distance. She should make it easily enough with an umbrella.

She made herself walk briskly toward the hotel, although the closer she got to it the more she felt like running in the opposite direction. She had purposely left a little late so that Farnham would be there ahead of her. The picture of herself sitting anxiously on the edge of a chair waiting for him didn't appeal to her. Also, the tea lounge of a quiet hotel was hardly what he would be used to. If he felt slightly out of his element, it would do her position no harm. However, when she arrived, he was comfortably seated at a table reading a newspaper, a pot of tea at his elbow.

When he saw her, he rose politely, but hardly with eagerness, and motioned her to a chair.

"Thank you for coming," he said. "Will you have something to eat? May I pour you some tea?"

"Just tea, thank you," Diana replied. She was neither thirsty nor hungry, but the cup would give her something to do with her nervous fingers. She watched as he filled her cup, his hands deft and sure. Anxious tremors have never troubled them, she thought. He no longer wore formal city clothes, and in his beautifully cut tweeds he looked even bigger and more formidable than on the previous day.

He sat back in his chair and looked at her without the least trace of warmth. Then, with no preamble, he said, "I believe you knew my brother quite well."

"Yes, but—" Diana stopped. She had been about to add "but not for very long." She must watch every word, must never let nerves hustle her into giving David Farnham any unnecessary information.

There was a short pause, and then Farnham continued. "That's why I've come to you. I've been winding up Jeremy's affairs, and I came upon a number of canceled cheques that were sent to you at regular intervals."

So that's how you found me, Diana thought. A man like him would have no trouble tracing her through the bank. Suddenly it came to her in a flash of hope that almost took her breath away. Was it possible...just possible that the money was all he was interested in? Did he think that the Diana Verney on the cheques had simply been a girlfriend of Jeremy's? Surely that was what he would be likely to think. His sort was probably used to buying anything, even friendship.

"I came to find out if my brother had an obligation to you that should be settled," he went on.

There it was again, Diana thought, a clear indication that he knew only of *her* existence. No mention of Kris...and, particularly, no mention of Noel. Relief swamped her.

His gray eyes, so like Jeremy's, were watching her face with impersonal speculation. In spite of herself Diana felt indignant. What right had he to assume that Jeremy had been keeping her? Then her common sense took over again. No one could really blame him for what he was thinking, and in a way he was right. For a time Jeremy had been keeping her, but for none of the common reasons, certainly none that he might suspect.

Yet she still felt resentful. "I assure you, Jeremy owes me nothing," she said stiffly. "But thank you for asking."

He looked slightly puzzled for an instant, as if he weren't quite sure of his ground, but it was a fleeting moment. This arrogant man would seldom be unsure of anything, she thought.

Then he went on. "You've had no cheques since Jeremy's death, of course. If they were an income that you were counting on, it might be arranged for them to continue for a strictly limited period...to the end of the year, let's say, to give you time to adjust your affairs."

Diana was dazed. On the surface his offer was generous, even kind, but it had been made in a tone of voice completely devoid of feeling. She stared at him, confused. What was he getting at? Then it dawned on her. He was warning her off. If she had it in mind to make some claim on his dead brother's estate, he was telling her clearly that it was definitely not on.

How dared he! Diana glared at him. "No, that will not be necessary. It was a—a private arrangement between Jeremy and me, and I prefer to keep it that way." She knew that if she kept this up he would think that she had been no more than an expensive call girl. But what did that matter? His opinion of her was of no consequence now that the baby was no longer in danger. She would end this interview.

Just as she was about to rise, there was a vivid slash of lightning, immediately followed by a tremendous crack of thunder. Diana jumped to her feet. Rain was drumming on the windows, and already water would be sloshing along the gutters. Noel! What if Mrs. Larkin were to stop for shelter under a tree?

Farnham was on his feet, too. "Are you afraid of thunder?"

"No, but I must get home at once." Diana seized her umbrella and, without another glance at him or anyone else, she made for the door.

She was battling the wind, gripping her umbrella hard and making little progress, when a car stopped a foot or two ahead of her. She barely noticed it until a strong hand closed on her forearm and a voice commanded, "Get in!" The door of a black Jaguar was open, and he hustled her toward it as he took her umbrella from her.

"I—I don't need a lift," she protested. "I live quite near."

"Will you *get* in!" he insisted angrily. "I don't enjoy getting wet."

Diana suddenly realized that if she didn't get into the car under her own steam, she would be tossed into it without further ceremony.

"Which way?"

"Straight ahead. It's only a few blocks." She didn't want to tell him exactly where she lived, but she knew that if David Farnham wanted any information about her, he would get it.

"Just drop me at this corner," she said.

"What number?"

"The corner will do perfectly well."

He gave her a look of exasperation. "The number!" he repeated.

"One twenty-five."

The Jaguar eased alongside the curb as he peered at the doors through the driving rain, and Diana gathered her coat around her, preparing to jump out quickly. Suddenly she heard an exclamation from Farnham, and she bent forward to look past him. She felt the bottom drop out of her stomach. Mrs. Larkin was struggling manfully to drag the baby carriage up the steep steps to the door, while the rain pelted down on her.

In an instant Farnham was beside the woman. "Go ahead and open the door," he ordered, and then picked up the carriage, baby and all, as if it were a toy.

Diana hurried after him, and Mrs. Larkin turned to her. "We got caught in the park by the storm, and it was better to come back than go on to my sister's," she said. She was out of breath and soaking wet but she laughed. "His Highness here thought it was all for his benefit, of course. And now I can see he's quite delighted to have you home. Just look at him!"

Noel was indeed looking delighted. The more company he had the better he liked it. He was pushing himself up and down, going through all his welcoming noises. Suddenly he became still as he sat up straight and lifted wondering brown eyes to David Farnham's face. They gazed at one another, as if each had found in the other something startling but of great importance.

Diana broke the silence. "Mrs. Larkin, could you look after Noel for a few more minutes? I'll be free then." Without a word she turned to the stairs and went up to her apartment. She could hear David Farnham's tread behind her, hear the menace in his every step. He said nothing and

once in her sitting room, with the door firmly closed behind him, Diana felt the ominous silence blanket her like a
fog. It tightened the knot in her throat and jangled her
nerves until she shook.

Farnham stood with his back to the door as if to cut off
her escape. She turned her head and looked into his face,
but it told her nothing. Then he lifted a hand and pushed
back heavy dark hair as if to clear his vision. "Diana," he
said, "this is no time for evasion. Is that my brother's
child?"

Diana saw a bitter twist to his mouth. Was it pain or disgust? But regardless of the consequences, she knew she
could not lie to him. For a moment she was tempted, but
Noel had rights, too, and having a connection to his father
was one of them.

"Yes," she said. "He is Jeremy's son."

Farnham walked to the window and stood with his back
to her. As she waited for him to speak, the truth suddenly
struck Diana with bitter force. His question had confirmed
that until a few moments ago he had never even suspected
the existence of Noel. She waited, trembling, for his reaction.

At last he swung around. "Diana, why didn't you or Jeremy tell someone in my family about the baby? I know I was
in Rio for the past three years, but my father was here. He's
no ogre."

You or Jeremy...? Diana's heart lurched. Still no mention of the baby's mother. As if a searchlight had swept
through the confused corners of her mind, Diana could see
that David Farnham was making a bigger mistake than ever.
And without meaning to he had offered her a way out of her
difficulties. He had taken it for granted that she, Diana, was
Noel's mother and as long as he went on believing that, she
would be in much less danger of losing the baby.

For a long time Diana couldn't say a word. She had too much to sort out, but at last she answered him. "Jeremy couldn't tell anyone. There was his wife to think of, you see."

"Yes, I do see." He paced up and down, pushing his hair back from his brow in his now-familiar gesture of exasperation. Then she saw a look of disgust wipe some of the incredulity from his face. It was clear that David Farnham would find it hard to make excuses for any man, even his brother, who would marry one girl while another was carrying his child. In spite of herself Diana felt some sympathy for him. She shouldn't let him suffer unnecessarily, and it wasn't entirely fair to Jeremy, either.

"Mr. Farnham," she ventured, "I—"

"Call me David," he broke in. "There is no possibility that we can be strangers now."

"Well, in fairness to Jeremy, you must listen to me." His eyes were on her face, and she drew a steadying breath. There was such a narrow line between saying enough and saying too much. "When your firm sent Jeremy to some faraway outpost about a year and a half ago, the baby was already on his way, but nobody knew about it."

"Nobody? Do you mean that literally?"

"Oh yes, quite literally." Diana kept her voice even. "By the time it was a certainty, Jeremy couldn't be reached, and your office said his mail was being held for his return."

"That would be true. It is common practice for anyone doing that tour. The tour includes so many inaccessible outposts that no one would have given the mail another thought."

"It didn't matter too much at first," Diana went on. "You see, it seemed certain that he would be back in plenty of time. How could anyone guess that he would—would marry so suddenly?"

"That was a shock to us, too," David assured her. "Jeremy had done such a good job for the firm in a lot of ungodly, uncomfortable places that my father told him to stop over in New York for a while as a sort of bonus. We were both impressed with how well he had taken hold of things. It was Jeremy's first really big job on his own. Certainly he stayed in New York for rather a long time, but no one expected that his vacation would end with a marriage."

Diana felt regret stir again as she remembered Jeremy, but she said nothing. What was there to say?

"And you?" For the first time a note of sympathy warmed his voice. "You waited for a message from him that never came."

"Yes," she admitted. She had waited ... waited and watched through her sister's weary hours of empty longing. She couldn't quite smother a sob as she remembered Kris's wistful eyes each time the postman had passed their door.

"I'm truly sorry." Farnham sat down near her, and Diana was surprised at the gentleness in his voice.

It was true that she had suffered, too, but she felt like a fraud. The only way she could accept his sympathy was by reminding herself that she was taking it for Kris.

David sat silent for some time, his head bowed, apparently lost in his own memories. Then he roused himself. "I know Jeremy was carefree and often thoughtless, but the idea of him treating two young women so shabbily at the same time is—is—" He threw his hands up as words failed him. "I'm deeply grateful to you for explaining how it happened, since it caused you, in particular, so much pain."

Diana was glad she had made the effort. She knew she must have sounded pretty cool, but that couldn't be helped. She had actually told no lies about Noel's birth, but she was letting David take it for granted that she was the baby's mother. That was something she would have to learn to live with. If she was to keep her promise to her sister, this might be the only way to do it.

True, David Farnham hadn't shown any marked interest in Noel, but if he should want to make difficulties, he would be a formidable adversary. Diana looked again at his handsome face, his fearless eyes, the confident lift to his chin, and shuddered at the thought of having to oppose him.

He interrupted her thoughts. "Diana, this is too big a load for you to carry alone. You must let me help you."

"I don't need help," she told him. "I can give Noel all he needs." She tried to speak decisively but her voice faltered. She had been doing her best to keep her emotions in check, but now she was beginning to feel the strain.

He sighed in exasperation. "Look, you've had a tough year," he said, "more than your fair share of trouble and sorrow...."

Diana knew he was offering her sympathy again, and she hardened herself against it. True, she'd had a tough year, the toughest of her life, but she'd made it. Noel was fine, her job was promising, and she had a decent place to live. That would do for now.

She threw back her head. "Single-parent families aren't uncommon these days," she said. "We'll get by."

"That's the point." His voice was firm. "Believe me, there's no need for a Farnham to just 'get by.'"

"You forget," she said with annoyance, "Noel is a Verney too."

"Oh, don't be a fool," he snapped. "Am I likely to forget that? At the moment I am simply trying to make one or two sensible suggestions in a situation I didn't expect."

"I see." Diana felt her temper rising. "You expected to meet a kept woman—one who would have had enough sense to avoid the consequences."

He glowered at her. "I admit there is a grain of truth in what you say. However, the fact remains, there *is* a 'consequence,' as you put it, and that consequence is my brother's son."

"What *you* seem to forget is that a mother is just as important as a father." She steeled herself to hold her voice steady. "Just leave us alone and be thankful that I am not asking you to shoulder any unexpected responsibilities."

He looked at her, his angry expression turning suddenly bleak. "I seem to have got off on the wrong foot with you, Diana. Will you believe that the last thing I want to do is to hurt either you or the boy? To me he is a Farnham, and he always will be, whether his parents were married or not. I hope, when some of the pain has gone, you will be able to think of things that way, too."

Diana felt a lump rise in her throat. Maybe he was kind underneath, she thought, but he was also strong. Too strong. If he should decide to *take* Noel, what chance would she have? But maybe she was just paranoid. So far the only thing he had said that should worry her was that he looked on Noel as a Farnham. He could hardly be blamed for that.... If anything, it was an admirable reaction. The trouble was that money, and lots of it, could buy almost anything—including a top-rank lawyer to argue about the guardianship of an orphaned baby. And that was why David Farnham must never find out that Noel no longer had a mother.

"Look," David said, interrupting her thoughts. "There is a lot we should talk about, but we both need a few hours to think first. Would you have dinner with me tomorrow evening? Perhaps by then I can come up with some suggestions that you would be willing to consider. In any case we must talk about Noel's future. Don't you agree?"

Diana wasn't willing to admit that there was any "must" about it, but she knew it would be sensible to avoid antagonizing him. If she was reasonably agreeable, perhaps David Farnham would continue to take the situation at face value.

"Probably you're right," she admitted, "but I'll have to check with Mrs. Larkin first to see if she can keep Noel for me." She was relieved when he left after telling her he would call her in the morning to see if she could get away, and to arrange a time for him to pick her up the next night.

Diana felt drained when he had gone. She went over every word of their conversation that she could remember, and she didn't think she had made any blunders. David's mistake about the mother of the baby had given her an unexpected advantage. To take a child away from an aunt was one thing, but to take it from a mother was much more difficult. If she could continue the pretense...

The evening shuffled by after she put Noel to bed, and the night was as bad as the one before. Diana was so tightly strung that sleep was impossible. At two in the morning she tossed out her last pillow with a groan of exasperation. She was as restless as she had been a good two hours before. She tried to think of something different, something comforting, but she soon gave that up, too. Midnight fantasies were all very well, but not when they brought her right back to David Farnham. The handsome face and imposing figure that drifted through her tattered half dreams reminded her all too vividly of him.... The fact that his menace had been replaced by an awareness of his exciting masculinity was very far from soothing.

Nevertheless, there was an unexpected satisfaction in the thought that she had agreed to meet him again.

CHAPTER THREE

NOEL'S USUAL DEMAND for attention prodded Diana awake early the next morning. "Look here, young man," she said, "one of these days I'm going to have to teach you the facts of life. For example, Sunday is a day of rest, R-E-S-T. Understand? The crack of dawn is strictly for the birds."

Noel, standing up in her lap, gave her a lopsided grin and a couple of healthy thumps, which was his way of showing approval.

"And another thing," she went on, ducking a right hook. "No gentleman hits a lady. What you need is a firm hand, one that will really teach you manners."

She caught her breath sharply. That came under the heading of true words spoken in jest. Would Noel need a stronger hand than hers one day? For a fleeting moment she pictured the big figure of David Farnham behind the tiny one of the baby. If he saw himself as a candidate for the job, how could she possibly oppose him? Perhaps after talking with him at dinner she would have a clearer idea of what the future might hold...or even of what she might want it to hold.

Late in the afternoon she handed Noel over to Mrs. Larkin, thanking her for agreeing to take Noel on a weekend and at such short notice. Then she gave some thought to what she would wear. She was perplexed. Here she was on two successive days thinking seriously about clothes. She hadn't been as interested in what to wear since college, and she wasn't sure that this was the time to start again. Still, a smart dress was a wonderful morale builder, and she certainly needed all the help she could get. David Farnham was coming for her at six sharp.

To go through her wardrobe was no great task since there was very little in it. She'd had to sell most of Kris's beautiful things, but there remained a very smart, deep blue silk suit that fortunately she had been able to keep. Its narrow, longish skirt and stylishly exaggerated top looked like nothing on a hanger, but on a woman's figure the subtlety of its cut suddenly took over. It flaunted nothing, but hinted at every feminine curve, every gentle hollow. For tonight its understated elegance would be exactly right.

She dressed with some satisfaction. At least she had all the right curves in the right places. Those above her waist were lush enough to be interesting, and those below tapered smoothly to long legs that had been whistled at since she was fifteen. She clustered the burnished waves of her hair over one shoulder and held them away from her face with a single pin. Then she deepened the blue of her eyes with a discreet shadow and heightened the pink of her cheeks and lips until their glow warmed the smooth contours of her face. As she took a last look at herself, she had to admit that the excitement of dressing for a man, even David Farnham, had returned the sparkle to her looks that had been missing for some time.

She watched as the black Jaguar turned into her street, and went down to meet it. She pulled the collar of her coat higher against the wind, but she knew that the shiver that shook her when she stepped toward David Farnham wasn't entirely due to the chill of the night.

As she settled into the glove-soft leather seat, he said, "I have arranged to have dinner at my house."

Diana was startled. She had accepted his invitation seeing in her mind a crowded restaurant. A private house was quite another matter. She glanced at his face, and one raised eyebrow and a cynical lift to the corner of his mouth told her that he hadn't missed her slight start of apprehension.

"Believe me, you have nothing to worry about," he said. "My housekeeper, as well as being an excellent cook, is an adequate chaperone."

"Thank you," she answered primly, not knowing whether to be annoyed or gratified. But his mention of the housekeeper was reassuring, and she did want to see his home. It would give her a chance to find out something of his background. The more she knew about him the better.

When they arrived it was too dark to see much of the house, but it was in an exclusive cul-de-sac, and Diana sensed that it was very large. Its Regency doorway was lighted by a pair of handsome carriage lamps, and the door was opened by a maid who helped Diana with her coat.

As the coat slipped from her shoulders her nerves tingled when she saw a flicker of interest in David's glance. It was as if he were seeing her for the first time...and her breath quickened slightly as their eyes locked for a moment. She was experienced enough to recognize that speculative, masculine look, the kind of look that told her he was aware of her as a woman. Then, with startling suddenness, it was gone. A shutter had come down, and now his eyes held only polite interest as he ushered her into the drawing room. It was as if he had turned off a light that might show more than he wanted to reveal. But the episode had been momentary, and perhaps she had only imagined it.

"Let me pour you a drink. A cocktail, vodka, sherry...?" he asked as he led her to a sofa by the fireplace.

"Sherry, please," she answered and looked about her with interest.

It was a nobly proportioned room but comfortable and welcoming. The great hearth almost filled one end of it, and at the opposite end was a pair of doors, probably opening onto a garden but now curtained against the cold night. The walls were paneled in a pale wood and were matched by a fine parquet floor. Rich carpets made pools of color in the soft light that came from silk-shaded lamps, and a great gilt-framed mirror over the fireplace echoed the flicker from the logs burning below.

"What a beautiful room!" Diana exclaimed as he handed her a drink.

"Yes, I think it is," he agreed. "It hasn't been changed much since Jeremy and I lived here as children. Of course, until we went away to school, we spent most of our time upstairs in the nursery at the top of the house. My parents live mainly in Scotland now, and the house became mine a few years ago."

It must indeed be a splendid house if the rest of it was like this, Diana thought, but how unusual that it should be occupied by a single man. Why had he no wife and family already established in it?

David interrupted her thoughts. "Where is your home?" he asked. "All Londoners, except the real Cockneys, seem to come from someplace else."

"I was brought up in Oxford," she answered, "but my parents were divorced years ago, and my father was appointed to an American university. He is an historian."

"How does he feel about Noel?" David asked. "He can't see much of him, surely, with so many miles between them."

"He doesn't know about Noel. I could see no reason to tell him since I felt he wouldn't be very pleased to have a fatherless grandson."

"I see."

Diana wondered if he really did see, or did he perhaps think she was ashamed to acknowledge an illegitimate child? Well, it was unimportant now, but she had told her father the exact truth about Kris's death—that Kris had died following a bad fall on the stairs.

David looked at her quizzically. "You are a bit of a loner, aren't you?" he said.

Diana supposed she was. She hadn't always been, but for the past few months Noel had taken up all of her time outside her working hours. Perhaps that was why, in spite of her fear of him, she was savoring the luxurious atmosphere of David Farnham's house. It certainly was a change from her usual environment.

David didn't seem to want any sort of serious discussion until after dinner, and Diana was glad to talk trivialities with him. Before long the maid announced dinner, and David showed her to the dining room.

The meal was what she would have expected... perfect cooking and perfect wine made even more splendid by the candlelight flickering on snowy linen, crested silver, delicate glass and a great display of flowers in the center of the round table. Diana did her best to forget her trepidation by feasting her eyes on the truly lovely table, but every now and then it surfaced in her. She reached for her wineglass, but she couldn't quite conceal the tremor in her fingers as she picked it up.

As she set it down again, David looked at her mockingly. "I'm not the Big Bad Wolf, you know. Why don't you relax?"

Diana's temper jerked to the surface. "As long as you remember I'm not Little Red Riding Hood," she answered coldly. Strangely enough, she thought she saw a flicker of amusement in his quick glance, but he made no further attempt to lighten her mood.

"Coffee in the drawing room?" he asked when they had finished eating.

"Yes, thank you, that would be nice," she said, and cautioned herself to be more civil. David Farnham had enough going for him without antagonizing him as well.

He motioned her to the same seat she'd occupied earlier and stood quietly for a moment looking down into the fire. Again, as she waited for him to speak, she saw in him the tough chairman of Farnham Industries. She shivered. Why on earth had she allowed herself to be brought here? A discussion was certainly necessary, but perhaps in a public place she would have felt less intimidated.

"Come, sit closer to the fire. I see you're cold. I should have poured you a coffee right away."

Well, she thought, if he had seen her shiver it was better that he thought it was from cold rather than from fear. She accepted the coffee but refused a cognac to go with it. She needed to keep a clear head if she was to hold her own with him.

David pulled forward an ottoman and sat on it, not far from her knees. He was gazing into the flames, and the firelight threw into relief the planes of his handsome face, the reflection gilding the outline of his profile and edging his sensual mouth. Then, as he turned his head and she looked into his eyes, she was aware for the first time of an underlying shadow in their depths, almost a sadness, and suddenly she wondered if she really had the right to come between this man and Noel.... It was a disturbing thought and she put it from her.

At last he spoke. "I hope I can convince you that I have no intention of trying to harm either you or your son. Every time I look at you I can almost feel you quaking. Why are you so afraid of me? I simply don't understand."

Diana made herself look at him coolly. "You are mistaken," she said. "I don't fear you, but I do fear the power of your money. You might as well know right now that it will never buy Noel."

His head lifted with a jolt. "That's unfair!" Anger snapped in his voice. "I don't attempt to buy people by any means whatsoever." He sprang to his feet and paced up and down for a minute. Then he swung around to face her. "Try to believe me, Diana. No court in the land would take a young child from its natural mother without a very good reason. And I don't want to take him from you. All I want is to make sure that, as a Farnham, he has everything he needs. Can't you believe that?"

She did at the moment, but the nagging question was still there. Would he be content to leave Noel with her if he ever found out the weakness of her position and the strength of his own?

"Jeremy would always have looked after his son," David insisted.

Diana wasn't so sure, but an argument about that would be pointless at this juncture. "Perhaps you are right," she said.

"Then will you go along with me regarding some things I would like to do for Noel?"

"Why should you *do* anything?" Diana asked. "You are not Noel's father. You are not obliged to—"

"Damn it!" David exploded. "What difference does it make now which Farnham pays for the baby—Jeremy or I?"

Diana's chin jerked up. "I see," she said icily as she jumped to her feet. "An unmarried mother shouldn't care what man makes an honest woman of her. Is that it?"

He glared at her for a moment, and then, strangely, she saw his shoulders droop slightly as he turned from her. Then he faced her again. "I'm sorry, Diana. Sometimes I forget what Jeremy's death must have meant to you."

For a moment David's unexpected sympathy touched her, and in her overwrought state she couldn't stop a tear from spilling over her eyelashes. He saw it at once and reached out to comfort her, and suddenly she was being held against his broad chest. She could hear the thud of his heart, feel the warmth of his body and smell the masculine nearness of him. His mouth was close to hers, and his breath fanned her cheek. She pushed him away but even as she did so, she knew that she had stayed in his arms a moment longer than she should have.

"It's—it's all right," she ventured. "I have been a little strung up the past few days."

"I can understand that," he said. "Sit down and I'll bring you a cognac now. You need it."

"Thank you," she said and took her place near the fire again as he went to fetch her drink. Her head was whirling, and she knew that her tension was only partly due to her anxiety about Noel. Much more disturbing was the sudden turmoil that the touch of this man had stirred within her.

They talked in generalities as she sipped her brandy, and she knew he was giving her time to pull herself together.

Finally he came to the point. "Will you consider letting the monthly cheques continue?"

She shook her head. "No—I don't really need them now. At Noel's age he wants very little and, thanks to my land-lady, I can spend as much time with him as any working mother."

"But that's the point. With a proper income you wouldn't need to work."

"Of course I would!" she exclaimed. "My work isn't just a job, you know."

"Isn't it?" he said. "Surely that small shop isn't enough for you. Wouldn't you be happier in a bigger one, a more important place?"

Diana laughed. "Good heavens, no! My employer is one of the best design jewelers in the country—in Europe for that matter. I assure you, I have my hands full."

He looked far from convinced, and suddenly it dawned on her that he had really no idea of what she did.

"David, I don't just sell those lovely things," she said. "I design and make quite a lot of them myself. It's what I have been trained to do."

"Well, I'll be—" He looked at her with surprise and reached out to take her hands. He gazed down at them, carefully running a thumb over the soft white skin and examining the delicate pink nails. Then he turned her hands over and examined the other side. "You mean, with these you saw and hammer and file and polish?"

She laughed a good-natured laugh. "Yes, and a good many other things, too. Come and see how it's done sometime if you like." The invitation was out before she quite realized she was making it. She didn't really enjoy being watched while she worked, but somehow she wanted so much to show this man. Show him what? She didn't quite know, but she did know that she wanted his approval, perhaps even his admiration.

"I will," he said, accepting the invitation with enthusiasm. "I might even acquire a personal jeweler, mightn't I? Think of what it could do for my social life. Broaden my horizons, as they say."

He smiled, and for the first time Diana saw real laughter in his face. She looked at him in surprise. A broad grin had pulled a deep dimple into each cheek, and his eyes danced. Until this moment she hadn't seen his face completely free of sadness or anxiety. Suddenly, like the sun breaking through, she had a glimpse of a gaiety and a reckless sense of fun that she hadn't suspected in him. For anyone who was fond of him, she thought, that smile would be well worth working for.

She noted that he wore no jewelry, and she wondered if, like so many men, he had a medallion around his neck, but she could see no outline of one through his evening shirt. It would be fun to design one for him, she thought. She could picture it...something very masculine, a heavy, yellow-gold disc with a heroic design...maybe Rhodian or Minoan. It would gleam amid short, curling hair on his chest, hair that was crisp under her hand and—she stopped. Her mind was wandering, wandering into unsafe places.

"You are miles away," he said, leaning closer. "What you've just told me puts an entirely new light on your work. Of course you must go on with it. A career is vastly different from a job."

They sat in silence for a short time, but when he spoke again she sensed a different note in his voice...a note that made the warning bells jangle in her head again.

"Diana," he began, "I know Noel is well looked after, and that he is in no real need of anything, but there are others who should be involved in his life, even though they don't know it yet. That's what I really need to talk to you about."

"Others?" Diana was startled. "You don't mean Jeremy's widow, do you," she asked.

"Good Lord, no! She's nice enough, and probably made a good wife for Jeremy, but she's young and pretty, and it won't surprise me at all if she's married someone else by this time next year. As a matter of fact, she has already gone back to America. No, I was thinking of my parents. You see, they have no other grandchildren, and the loss of Jeremy was a terrible blow, particularly to my mother. Noel could be a great comfort. It would be like getting part of Jeremy back. Shouldn't you take that into consideration? As for my father—at last he has a grandson, a grandson who might someday head Farnham Industries. Think what that would mean to him.''

For a moment Diana wondered if this was a ploy to win her sympathy, but the serious look on his face told her there was a great deal more to it. ''But surely,'' she said tentatively, ''surely you haven't given up the idea of marriage for yourself and—and children of your own and—''

His voice overrode hers, harsh and uncompromising. ''I should explain that I have already had one unsuccessful marriage and I have no intention of chancing another.''

Diana was about to offer some fairly innocuous reply, but a glance at his grim expression stopped her.

''Believe me,'' David went on more naturally. ''I'm not trying to force you or even coax you into anything to do with Noel's future at the moment, but perhaps if we could see eye to eye in certain things, between us we might find some way to make this situation happier for everyone.''

Diana felt torn apart. She was desperately afraid of losing the baby, but at the back of her mind there lingered a bigger and blacker fear: if anything were to happen to her, what would become of Noel? He was so alone in the world, and she was bone tired of meeting every crisis, making every decision, on her own. If David Farnham were to truly become her friend, her burden would be considerably lightened.

David was watching her, making no move to influence her, but she could sense the depth of his anxiety. Up to this point Diana had been thinking principally of Noel's relationship with her and what it meant to her personally. Now she had been forcibly made aware of the little boy's great importance to the Farnham family. She shuddered—already she felt almost overwhelmed.

She looked at David, but he had already said his piece. It was now up to her. She had nothing to fall back on except instinct, and for what it was worth, instinct was shoving her in David's direction. She *wanted* to know this man better; she *wanted* the assurance of his support; she *wanted*— She was no longer sure exactly what it was she wanted of him, but she knew she didn't want to put him out of her life forever...not now.

"Well—" she cleared her throat "—we might at least see if we can reach some understanding about Noel's future."

And that's as much as I can take right now, she thought, and was glad when he took her home almost at once.

LATER, IN HER APARTMENT, she thought that perhaps she hadn't done too badly after all. She had committed herself to nothing more than further talks with David, a commitment that wasn't entirely disagreeable.

Nevertheless she did not drift off into a contented sleep that night, either. Her mind was too full of disturbing contrasts...David's beautiful drawing room with her minute apartment...his handsome dining room and the scrubbed counter in her kitchen. She had known that he was a wealthy man, but to see and touch the lovely things he lived with every day shook her confidence. Did she really have the right to shut off the baby from all that? Was she holding on to Noel for purely selfish reasons, just because she couldn't bear the thought of being without him? Was she right to suppose that no one else could give him love but her?

She wasn't unduly impressed either by David's appeal for sympathy on his parents' behalf. If he wanted grandchildren for them, what was wrong with supplying a few himself? He certainly looked capable of it, given the usual cooperation, and he didn't look as if he would ever be short of that.

She gave her pillow an exasperated shove.

Much later she fell into an uneasy sleep, only to dream about a smiling man coming toward her through a bevy of children, a golden jewel gleaming on his broad, bare chest, and as her fingers went out to touch it, he moved away... tantalizingly beyond her reach. "Wait! Wait for me," she cried, but he disappeared, and she awoke feeling a desolate sense of loss.

She knew that all these disturbed nights were getting her down, but what could she do about them? They were simply a reflection of her state of mind, and she felt battered and bewildered. Her biggest worry was the fact that any decision she made would color the whole of Noel's future. He wouldn't always be an infant, and she felt as if she were holding his life between her palms. She needed advice but had nowhere to turn for it. If only she had a friend like— well, like David Farnham himself... experienced, knowledgeable, concerned. And what made her think he had these qualities? Then she remembered that he had given her the opportunity to get to know him better. She resolved now to take it.

The thought was comforting enough to soothe her into a much-needed sleep.

CHAPTER FOUR

DIANA HAD EXPECTED TO HEAR from David very soon, but nearly a week had passed with no word from him. Somehow she was disappointed, and that was strange, considering how his sudden appearance had disrupted her life. But maybe this reaction was a healthy one. It was natural for her to feel nervous about his interest in Noel but there was no need for her to get paranoid about it. Certainly if he stayed away from them she might lose some of her anxiety, but she would also lose the stimulation of his company....

For the first time since coming to London she wondered if she had been too long without a man in her life.

At that moment the phone rang. "Is it all right to call you at the shop?" David asked, and she felt her spirits lift at the sound of his voice.

"Oh, of course," she answered.

"If you are free on Sunday will you have lunch with me and spend the rest of the day at the house? The weather isn't really good enough for me to offer to take you anywhere, but it might be pleasant just to sit by the fire and talk."

Diana would have loved to accept his invitation, but it was too bad that he had chosen Sunday. "Oh, I'm afraid I can't, David," she said. "Sunday is Mrs. Larkin's day off too, and she won't be able to take Noel. She had him last Sunday, and I can't ask her to do it again so soon."

"Good!" he exclaimed, pleasure warming his voice. "Let's have him at the house. The staff has to meet him sometime, you know."

Diana couldn't really see why they did, but she didn't want to cross David so soon. After all, she had promised to try to get along with him. "Well, if you think it will be all right," she ventured.

"Of course it will," he declared. "I hope that someday he will think of my house as his home, too."

Diana's heart took a dive. David was not being as casual about Noel as she had hoped. He was obviously already way ahead of her in thinking about the baby's future. She'd had to content herself with making sure that Noel was properly looked after, more or less on a day-to-day basis, but David could afford to take a much longer view. His mention of his house made her wonder if he already saw himself as Noel's guardian, and if so, where did that leave her?

"I'll collect you whenever you like," David went on. "You can bring everything you'll need with you."

Diana was still dubious, but she could think of no acceptable excuse for keeping Noel away from him. Maybe later she would find some way of keeping them apart. In the meantime the best thing she could do would be to concentrate on being reasonably friendly and cooperative.

Somehow that thought was no longer unwelcome.

When Sunday came Diana dangled a couple of small woolen suits in front of Noel. "Well, which is it to be?" she asked. "You should have a choice. After all, this is the first time you have gone to visit anybody."

"Glub!" Noel said helpfully.

"I think you're right," Diana agreed. "Blue is your best color."

She dressed him with pleasure. He really was a beautiful little boy. His hair was growing darker, she noticed, as she brushed a small coxcomb to the top of his head. Probably he was going to be dark like the Farnham men, but he would always have the velvet-brown eyes of his mother. If he inherited the good looks of both his parents he would be devastating when he grew up.

David would be along shortly, and she took a last look at herself as well. Knowing she would be likely to spend a good deal of time on the floor with Noel, she had put on a dark red pantsuit with one of Kris's Hermés scarves tucked into its neckline. The scarf had probably cost more than everything else she had on put together, she thought with amusement, but it certainly did a lot for the outfit.

Just as she finished dressing, the door buzzer sounded. She pressed the button to let David in, and in a few seconds he was up the stairs.

She laughed as she watched him gaze down at Noel, who was clinging to the rail of his playpen and returning David's examination with interest. Both faces were solemn, and then, as if on cue, they grinned at each another. David dropped to his haunches and studied the small face.

"I'm David," he announced. "David...David. Go ahead, try it."

"Ah-dah-dah-dah-dah!" Noel said obligingly.

"Listen to that! He's having a go at it! That's a bright boy, you know."

Diana did know, but she was amused by David's assurance.

Like Noel, David too was wearing blue. No city clothes this time. A light blue shirt accentuated the glow of health that warmed his skin, and she could glimpse the exciting shadow of small crisp curls on his chest under the vee of the shirt's open neckline. Her eyes traveled down to the tight jeans clinging to his long thighs like a second skin and hinting at the swell of masculinity they concealed. Diana felt her

breath come faster and caught her ripe lower lip between her
teeth. He really did have everything, everything a woman
could desire. So why wasn't there a wife to appreciate it all?
Maybe he hadn't had time yet to recover from the marriage
he had spoken of, or perhaps he just enjoyed playing the
field, she thought. And who could blame him? With that
kind of machismo he would never be short of playmates.

"What do you have to bring? Just that?" He pointed with
surprise to her canvas carryall. "Then I can take that as well
as Noel," he said.

Diana could see he was itching to pick up the baby, and
decided to humor him. "I'll take the bag," she said, "but
I'd be glad if you would take Noel. He squirms a bit, which
is nerve-racking going down the stairs."

Diana saw his smile broaden as he bent over the playpen
and said, "Okay, Hotshot. Squirm away!" As he took Noel
in his arms for the first time, the look of tenderness in his
face astonished her. It was quite unexpected in such a
worldly man. Maybe she had been unjust to suppose that he
saw Noel as just another Farnham possession.

Diana followed them downstairs, and her jaw dropped as
she stepped out the front door. She hadn't seen David arrive, and she wasn't prepared for the gleaming limousine
with its uniformed chauffeur.

"Oh, I forgot to tell you." David looked slightly embar-
rassed. "I didn't know what paraphernalia you would need
for Noel, so I brought the big car. Are you sure you've got
everything?"

Diana got her breath back. "That car would take his cot
and playpen as well," she remarked, laughing.

"Just say the word...."

"No, no, we've got everything he needs," she assured
him.

"Well, if you're sure..."

"I am." Everything the baby owned in the world, she thought, would go into one corner of that elegant car.

Diana got in first. The elderly chauffeur was holding open the door and as David, carrying the baby, reached him, she saw a look of deep feeling pass between the two men. She was surprised at this reaction but as they started on their way, David explained.

"Diana, I hope you won't be upset about this, but I felt I had to tell Mrs. Rogers, my housekeeper, about Noel."

For a passing moment Diana was annoyed that he hadn't asked her first but, after all, why should he? Surely he was free to tell anyone anything he chose.

"You see," David went on, "Mrs. Rogers worked for us when I was born and came back to us as nanny when Jeremy came along six years later. In the meantime she had married my father's chauffeur—" he nodded toward the driver "—and they have been with us ever since."

Diana suddenly realized that she felt relieved. She had known that the staff had to believe that she was Noel's mother, but for some reason she hadn't wanted them to assume that David was the father, which they might very well have done. She didn't try to think it through. She just knew that she didn't want anyone to believe that she'd had a hole-in-corner affair with David.

"No," she said, "I don't mind at all." She had seen Mrs. Rogers on her previous visit, and it had been obvious that she was a power in the household.

The front door opened the minute they reached the house, and Diana suspected that Mrs. Rogers had been watching for them. David marched straight in and handed Noel to the housekeeper. "Just give her a minute with the baby, won't you?" he asked Diana, and she was touched by the soft note of appeal in his voice. This was certainly his day for surprising her.

In a few minutes, almost before Diana and David were properly settled in the drawing room, Mrs. Rogers came in with Noel. She was smiling, but Diana could see traces of tears. "He's a beautiful baby, madam, and big for his age, too. Mr. David says he is just nine months old."

"Yes, he'll be a year old on Christmas Eve. That's why he's called Noel."

"Then he'll be a fine big man, I shouldn't wonder. Just like—" She stopped.

"Just like his father," David finished for her calmly.

Diana was startled at first, but then she realized that again David had done the right thing. It was kindness to speak openly to the woman about the baby's father since he had been her special care.

"Now what are we to do with him, Mrs. Rogers?" David asked. "He can't walk yet but he can crawl. We don't want to lose him."

"Well, there's the nursery, Mr. David."

"But that's so far away."

"Then how about the old baby carriage in the basement?" Mrs. Rogers asked. "We could bring it up here. It would be just the thing for him."

"Mrs. Rogers, that carriage is about as old as I am," David declared.

"Not *about*, Mr. David. Exactly as old! I remember when your father bought it."

Diana laughed and teased, "A cherished antique, no doubt."

"I'm not sure I care for the 'antique' bit," David said, grinning, "but I'm quite willing to go along with the 'cherished.' Well, let's have it up and see if Hotshot approves. We can tell him about this when he buys his first Jaguar, can't we, Diana?"

Diana shivered, but with pleasure this time. There was something reassuring about being included in plans for the distant future.

David was back shortly, pushing an old but elegant navy blue pram. Its perfect condition spoke of loving care. Suddenly Diana remembered the nannies she saw daily in Hyde Park, convoying plump babies in carriages just like this one. She had coveted one for Noel but had comforted herself with the thought that at least he would never be looked after solely by a paid servant. He would always be surrounded by love as long as she had anything to do with him.

"Well, will it do?" David cut into her thoughts.

"Do? It's lovely!" Diana said, and watched David roll his eyes heavenward as Mrs. Rogers nodded in agreement.

"No telling what women will think beautiful," he sighed.

"It will be just the thing, madam," said Mrs. Rogers. "Just leave it to me. There are plenty of pillows and covers to go with it upstairs."

"Why don't you go up too, Diana, and have a look at the nursery," David suggested. "There might be other things up there that Noel could use. I'll look after him while you're gone."

Diana had the feeling that he was dying to have the baby to himself. It was unexpected in such a sophisticated man, but she had noticed that every time he looked at Noel his face lit up.

"Well, if you're sure you can manage," she said. "I would like to see more of this lovely house."

She found that the nursery took up a major part of the top floor of the house. It had a large, sunny, happy-looking playroom with an adjoining double bedroom and bathroom. Across the corridor was a complete suite for the nanny.

As she glanced into the sitting room, Diana's eye fell on a photograph of the two Farnham brothers. Jeremy was much as she remembered him, but she had to look twice to make sure that the other joyous young man with the wicked gleam in his eyes was really the stern David. Each was carrying a tennis racquet and had his free arm thrown about his brother's shoulder. They were laughing heartily; even the Labrador at their feet seemed to be grinning into the camera. It was such a happy picture that Diana couldn't help smiling back at it.

"I wish you could have known them then," the housekeeper said behind her. "That's how I remember them. They were always so full of fun."

"It's a lovely picture. Was it taken very long ago?" Diana asked.

"Let me see, now. About four years ago, I should think. Yes, it was just before...just before Mr. David got married."

The housekeeper turned to go out of the room, but Diana had the strong impression that she had been going to say more and had stopped herself. Diana could respect that. Someone who had worked for half a lifetime in a household like this wasn't likely to gossip about the family. Yet there had been something, Diana was sure, something that the woman wanted to tell her. Could it have been about David's marriage?

Mrs. Rogers went to a cupboard in the hall and then came back to Diana again, her arms full of small baby blankets and pillows. "Plenty here as you can see, madam," she said, her voice unnaturally husky. "I never thought they would be wanted again."

Diana saw a tear splash down the woman's cheek, and she stepped forward quickly. "Sit down for a minute, Mrs. Rogers. Here—" she pulled forward a chair "—I'll fetch a glass of water."

When she returned from the small nursery kitchen, the housekeeper looked a little more composed, but Diana saw her hand shake as she took the glass.

"I'm sorry, madam. I think it was just the sight of the baby things again so soon after meeting the little one downstairs that upset me. I'm not given to tears, madam."

"I'm sure you're not, Mrs. Rogers," Diana soothed. "This has been a pretty upsetting time for all of us, you know."

The woman wiped her eyes and sat for a moment, the baby things held against her breast as if for comfort. Diana could almost feel her agitation. Suddenly, as if she had come to a decision, she lifted her head and looked straight at Diana.

"Madam, I think I should tell you," she said, looking worriedly into Diana's face. "There's no one else to do it, you see. Lady Farnham may not be back for months, and poor Mr. David, he...he...well, when he told us about the baby it was the first time I saw him looking really happy in years. I want you to know the truth about that business, just so you won't let anything go wrong between him and the little one. He's not *really* the sort of man to get married one year and divorced the next."

Diana was startled. She felt mean about encouraging the housekeeper to talk, but it was fairly clear from her agitation that what she wanted to say was something more than backstairs gossip.

"Mrs. Rogers, please believe me," she said quietly, "the most important thing in my life is the baby. If you have anything to tell me that could concern his future, then please don't hold back."

"Well, to tell you the truth, it's Mr. David's happiness that concerns me most. I'm sure you will understand that."

Diana nodded and waited. Surely the more she knew about David Farnham the better.

"Well, it was his marriage, you see. It was a mistake from the start. Mr. Jeremy did try to warn him, you know. I heard him often. Then one night he said, 'You're not going to *marry* her, are you, David? None of the other men in her life thought they had to.' And Mr. David hit him." The housekeeper turned pale at the memory.

Diana wasn't entirely surprised. There was an aura of contained violence in David....

"That was the only real quarrel I ever knew them to have," continued Mrs. Rogers.

"Don't go on if it upsets you," Diana said.

"Better you should hear it all, madam, now that I've started," she said determinedly, and Diana agreed. It would be better to know the facts than to keep wondering about them.

"Mind you, that woman was beautiful," Mrs. Rogers went on, "and she had plenty of money. She was no gold digger, I'll say that for her. No, it was men that she went after, and Mr. David was the best of them. But I knew that marriage wouldn't last. That's why I stayed on when Sir Edwin gave Mr. David this house. Nothing else would have persuaded me to keep house for that woman."

"How long did the marriage last?" Diana asked.

"Oh, just about a year, but it didn't take that long for Mr. David to know he had made a mistake."

Diana heard a bitter note in the housekeeper's voice. "Well, I suppose David must be over it by this time," she said, trying to make an innocuous remark.

"Oh, madam, I sometimes wonder if he will ever be over it."

Diana was startled. "Was it really that bad?"

"The worst! Parties, parties, parties! And Mr. David tried.... I think he blamed himself for tying her down too soon. He was so patient you wouldn't believe it, and then she found she was pregnant."

"Pregnant!" Diana was stunned. David had never mentioned a child. "But what happened to the baby?"

"Well you may ask, madam! Mr. David was so happy—" A sob shook the housekeeper again. "That hussy said she wasn't ready for a string of children. She refused to have it, and Mr. David didn't know what she was up to until after it was done."

"Oh, poor David!"

"Yes, it was just like something had died inside him instead of in her. Then one night I heard her screaming at him. Why was he going on and on about a brat that even *she* wasn't sure was his?"

Diana was shattered; she was too shocked to say a word.

"That was the last straw," Mrs. Rogers said. "Mr. David just walked straight out of the house and never came back until she was out of it for good."

They both sat silent for a moment. "Thank you for telling me, Mrs. Rogers," Diana said finally.

The housekeeper wiped her eyes. "Well, as I said, madam, there's nobody else to tell you. Maybe the baby downstairs will bring back some happiness here. Mr. David deserves it, for there never was a kinder man. No child could be in better hands."

Diana was a little alarmed that the housekeeper was taking it for granted that David was to be Noel's protector, but wasn't that what David wanted, too? And was she, Diana, completely against the idea? Perhaps she should consider some kind of compromise. She followed the housekeeper downstairs. She had certainly been given plenty to think about. She understood better the unexpected strength of David's affection for Noel, and his lack of a wife as well.

Diana found David and Noel in the drawing room, David stretched out on a sofa and the baby sitting happily on his chest. They were holding an animated conversation intelligible only to themselves, and as Diana watched the man's obvious delight in the little boy, her heart went out to him as she thought of his stormy, unhappy marriage. Could she deprive him of his young nephew, too, when he had so cruelly lost his own child?

Then, when Mrs. Rogers came in with an offer to take Noel for a little while, Diana handed him over, and David laughed when the woman had gone. "She's probably dying to show Noel off to the rest of the staff," he said.

"How many are there?" Diana asked.

"Only two more at the moment... Anna who is German, and Polly who is a real cockney. Incidentally, Polly has several grown-up children. With her experience, she might be useful if you need someone to look after Noel occasionally."

Diana felt again that slight stir of trepidation. This household could all too easily absorb a baby—and she wondered if she was getting in too deep and far too fast.

Soon Mrs. Rogers came back with a sleepy-looking Noel. "I think he's about ready for a nap now, madam. Shall I put him into the carriage?"

"No, I think I'll hold him for a few minutes," Diana said. "He hasn't seen much of me today."

The baby was already drowsy and David looked down at him in Diana's lap. "What he needs is a lullaby," he said, moving across the room, and in a few moments the opening strains of the "Moonlight Sonata" stole softly through stillness.

Diana hadn't noticed the music center earlier because it was housed in a section of the bookcases, but now she could see a fine collection of records and tapes.

David relaxed into a deep chair opposite Diana and as the heavenly music folded around them, his eyes rested on the baby and then lifted to her. Diana saw his strong face soften into a smile as his eyes wandered over the little figure resting against her breast, the pale satin of the cushions behind her, and the flicker of the firelight on her face and hair. "You make a lovely picture, the two of you," he said softly, and Diana was surprised at the unexpected vulnerability in his face.

She remembered again Mrs. Rogers's story and her heart went out to him. He seemed to have so much, but what he didn't have was painful enough to create that shadow of sadness behind his eyes.

As the music ended she said, "That was lovely, and what splendid reproduction. I've never heard better."

"Yes, it's good," he agreed. "I'm pleased with that stereo. I think it's the best I've had yet. Do you enjoy listening to music?" he asked eagerly.

"Very much." Little did he know, she thought. For months and months the music from her small radio had been her only pleasure, her one escape from grim reality. She had had no money to spare for any other form of entertainment.

She saw David's face light with enthusiasm. "Look here, could we give Noel back to Mrs. Rogers and listen for a while?"

Diana stared. This was a side of him she had never seen before. "That would be heavenly, but we don't have to worry about Noel. We can just put him in the carriage and wheel him into the hall. He'll sleep for hours."

"Good. I haven't listened to music for a long time. Too long. What shall we start with? Mozart?"

"What could be better?"

In a moment he had put on a symphony that she knew well, and Diana felt her whole body respond to the exciting *br-rrm*, *br-rrm*, *br-rrm* of the opening bars. David's music system really was exceptional. The reproduction was as near as one could come to hearing a live performance and as the sounds of a great orchestra surged through the firelit room, Diana let her head fall back against the soft cushions, and closed her eyes. All the raw edges of her tired nerves were smoothed away by the lovely sound, and she let herself relax under its caress.

David was contentedly slumped in a chair and as the last strains of the Mozart faded, he stretched languidly. "Wonderful!" he said. "Music like that makes your troubles seem bearable for a while, doesn't it?"

With an effort Diana pulled herself together and warned herself not to get too comfortable with David Farnham. "Yes, that was exciting," she agreed, "but I'm not sure that performance is quite as good as the one von Karajan did with the Berlin Philharmonic."

His eyebrows lifted in surprise, and they listened to more music and squabbled amiably about various performances for quite some time. Occasionally she caught an amused glint in his eye that made her wonder if he was intentionally trying to strike a spark from her. But it was fun, and Diana enjoyed watching him come to life—an echo of the teasing, smiling man she had seen in the photograph upstairs.

Then he watched her with a grin as Placido Domingo broke her heart with the "Flower Song" from *Carmen*.

As the great tenor's seductive voice drifted around them, David dropped on the sofa beside her, and she could feel the intimacy of his nearness. He leaned back and stretched his

long arms along the back of the sofa. She knew it was a
natural gesture for a big man, but she was uneasy, too aware
of him. He seemed completely intent on the superb voice,
and while Diana's breath came faster, David's was slow and
deep.

She felt him turn to look at her. His eyes searched hers,
and as his arm slid down across her shoulders she felt its
warmth burn through her. His other arm came around her
and as she felt herself gathered into him, every nerve in her
body seemed to reach out to answer his demand. As the
velvet voice on the disk whispered "Kiss me, kiss me, and
make all my dreams come true," his lips covered hers with
masterful intensity. She opened her own to the hunger of
him and savored his mouth until it scorched a path to the
hollows of her neck. His fingers reached to undo her scarf
and suddenly, as they touched the silk of her skin, he thrust
away from her and jumped to his feet.

"Oh, no, Diana. I never meant that to happen," he said.
"Believe me."

His words stung. She knew all too well that the embrace
hadn't been just his doing. She could still feel the tumult of
her own response, and she was thankful that he couldn't
know the turmoil that his kiss had stirred within her. It had
surprised her, and she wondered how she could possibly
have such feelings for a man who, as far as she was concerned, hadn't even existed two or three weeks ago. Or had
David suspected, before she knew it herself, that such fires
smoldered beneath her cool composure? Then she told herself that their passion had been no more than an accident
brought on by their proximity and the stimulating music.

She knew it was up to her to get back some remnant of
common sense, and she hoped he would not dwell on the
warmth of her response. She was sure the whole episode had
been no more than a lapse in restraint between two warm-

blooded—and probably love-hungry—people. And why
didn't that idea bring her comfort? she wondered.

"I know you didn't mean it," she answered at last, as
coolly as she could. Nevertheless she couldn't say "Neither
did I," for the truth was that, as his lips found hers, she
knew that she would answer that kiss, and more . . . much,
much more!

There was a sound at the door and the maid, Anna, announced dinner. Diana was relieved, and she could see that
David, too, was grateful for the interruption.

Shortly after dinner she asked him to take her home. He
did so without argument, and she hoped he didn't misun-
derstand her need to leave. She wasn't running away from
him; she simply felt she was at the end of her strength. It had
been a disturbing day, and she didn't want to make any further mistakes out of sheer nervous exhaustion.

When they reached her door David carried Noel upstairs
for her, and as she took the baby she said, "Thank you,
David. You were wonderful with him. It was good for him
to see you. He doesn't see many men."

David looked down at the infant. "Well, if he's going to
look to me as a shining example, I'd better mend my ways,
hadn't I?"

She knew he was offering her a sort of apology. "Oh, I
don't think you would lead him very far astray, David," she
said.

"Thank you. I'll keep that in mind." Then, with a part-
ing glance at the sleeping baby and a quiet good-night, he
was gone.

Later she thought over the whole afternoon. It had held
several surprises, not the least being the depth of her own
response to David's lovemaking. It had been completely
unexpected; nevertheless his arms about her and his mouth
on hers had seemed the most natural thing in the world.

Then she remembered his agitation when he'd broken away from her. Had he, too, been really disturbed? Had he felt more than just the casual urge to make a pass at an available female? Deep in her heart she knew she was already longing to see David Farnham again.

But not just Noel's uncle.

David Farnham, the man!

CHAPTER FIVE

THE NEXT MORNING when Diana arrived for work, Gian-Carlo greeted her with a knowing smile. She was reminded immediately of his harmless love for romantic intrigue, and also that he could find it almost anywhere. What was he up to this time? she wondered when she saw his smile deepen. "So you haven't the boyfriend, yes?" he said, every word oozing disbelief.

"No. I mean yes—yes, I haven't the boyfriend, no." Diana laughed, shook her head and watched his eyebrows climb toward his hairline.

"So, from the best flower shop in London he sends you this just for fun, no?" He paused for effect and then, with the flourish of a stage magician, produced from behind his back a long, ribbon-tied box.

Diana gasped. Even as florists' boxes went, this one was large. She lifted the lid and caught her breath at the great mass of American Beauty roses. Their scent filled the shop as she picked up the card that lay on top. It said only "David," and she stooped to cool her cheek against the satin of the luscious petals. Gian-Carlo pursed his lips, gave her a satisfied nod and went off to his workroom with a shrug that said no further words were necessary.

If this was an apology for yesterday's kiss, Diana thought, David didn't know how unnecessary it was. She knew perfectly well that she could have avoided that kiss, had she really wanted to. Could have, yes, but it had been the very last thing she had wanted to do at that moment.

She put the roses in water, admiring each lovely bloom, and then settled at her worktable. She chose a piece of hand polishing she had started on Friday. It was a routine job and would leave her mind free to go its way, for she knew she had a lot to think through.

For the first time since she had come to London she was remembering, and savoring, the feel of a man's arms about her, the sheer pleasure of masculine strength and the heady intimacy of a lingering kiss. Almost with surprise she realized that she had missed the excitement and the physical nearness of a man in her life. She'd had far too many other things on her mind since Kris's death to think about men, and now here was one pushing his way into her emotions. And not just any man, either. This was the one man whom she should be looking at with cool detachment. Should be, but wasn't.

She remembered the impact he had made on her that very first morning when he had come into the shop to find her. She remembered, too, trying to push away the sudden interest she'd felt. Now that she knew just how dangerous he could be to her, she should be even more anxious to keep him at a distance. But it didn't seem to be working that way. Nowadays the thought of him kindled a warm glow inside her that melted her fears when she should be wishing that he hadn't come into her life at all.

It wasn't that she wanted to keep men at arm's length. She had had her share of boyfriends at college, but she had never been really intimate with any of them. She remembered wondering once if she was being too prudish and, as usual, she'd turned to her sister for advice, particularly about the more physical side of dating. She could still hear Kris's hearty laugh.

"Look, darling," Kris had said, "this is once when big sister is not much use to you. You'll have to make your own rules here. For me that sort of thing has to be a bit more than just a 'roll in the hay,' but you'll have to set your own standards. The important thing is to *have* standards . . . and to stick to them."

Diana hadn't found that too difficult, for no man had come along who had held more than just plain sex appeal for her . . . no man, that is, until David Farnham. In exasperation Diana shook her head and sighed.

With an effort she brought her attention back to her work. That, at least, had never failed her, and she knew that Gian-Carlo was becoming increasingly pleased with her. Already he had promised that if she continued to do as well as she was now doing, he would offer her a permanent place in his business at the end of her apprenticeship. Reasonably soon she should be able to support herself and Noel in real comfort—without the help of anybody. In the meantime they were managing well enough on what she was earning.

When David telephoned her later in the week, she still hadn't sorted out her feelings, but she accepted his invitation to go out with him on the coming Saturday afternoon. Maybe if she got to know him better, the situation would become clearer to her. She wanted to be prepared for any action he might take regarding Noel, even though at the moment there was no way she could guess what he might do. She simply *had* to know him better, she repeated to herself, which didn't necessarily mean becoming more intimate with him. She told herself that seeing more of David was the sensible thing to do, but she had to admit that the "sensible thing" was seldom so attractive.

"Any particular place you would like to go?" he asked as they got into his car on Saturday afternoon.

"No, your choice will be fine." She smiled. "Noel's with Mrs. Larkin, so I'm free for the whole day."

"Then what about a little way out of town for a change?"

She glanced at him. There was a glint in his eye that made her wonder what he was up to, but she agreed. "All right," she said. If he was planning something, she would know about it soon enough.

As they started off Diana felt a rush of pleasure at being with such an attractive man. She had to admit that he was the most devastatingly good-looking man who had ever taken her anywhere. She couldn't think of a single girl she knew who wouldn't be thrilled to the core to have a date with David. But that jarred her into wondering what right she had to be sitting here beside him. Would she be in the lush Jaguar if David had just happened to meet her somewhere? At a party, maybe? After all, as just herself she had nothing special to offer. As Noel's mother it was quite a different story. For a moment depression swept her, and then she shook herself free of it. Why spoil what could be a pleasant day by worrying over things she could do nothing about?

She looked at him again. No formal city clothes this time. A gray Harris tweed sports coat sat comfortably on his broad shoulders, and cavalry twill trousers hugged his long legs. A pigskin waistcoat was buttoned over a pale shirt and a boldly-patterned bow tie added the right dash of color to his dark good looks.

"Will I do?" David asked, raising an eyebrow as he caught her inspection. "If there is anything you don't like just mention it and I'll take it off right away," he said with a quizzical smile.

Diana shook her head. "You're beautiful, my dear," she quoted with a laugh.

"I know," he agreed with mock smugness. "My mother has been telling me that for years."

"Has she? Tell me about her." Diana had avoided asking anything about his family, but now she felt it would be a good thing to know at least a little.

"You will meet her one of these days, but at present she's on a long cruise with my father. The shock of Jeremy's death was very hard on her, and my father is keeping a close eye on her health. He's as much in love with her now, I think, as on the day they were married, and she is just as devoted to him. I don't suppose that sort of thing happens very often, but with them..." He shrugged as if there was nothing more to be said.

Diana wondered if that was what he had expected of his own marriage. If so, the disappointment must have been doubly shattering. "When do you expect them back?" she asked.

"Oh, not for some time. I think my father will want to keep my mother in a mild climate until the worst of the winter is over."

They drove in silence for a while until Diana, growing a little impatient, asked, "Where are we going?"

"Just another few miles," he said.

She noticed at once that he hadn't really answered her question. Apparently he had some sort of surprise up his sleeve, and she decided to play along since he was in such a happy mood. He seemed to have put last Sunday out of his mind, and it was high time she did the same.

They passed miles of small suburban houses, each with its handkerchief of front lawn neatly fenced and gated. Then they made a turn up a short hill and were suddenly in another world, a world of impressive houses, wide gardens and fine trees.

David stopped the car by a village green. "There! What do you think of that?"

"What a lovely place!" Diana exclaimed. "But where are we?"

"You've no idea?" he asked with a smile.

"No."

"This is Harrow. Harrow School."

"You mean *the* Harrow?" she asked, wide-eyed. "Where all those great men were educated? Men like Lord Byron and Winston Churchill and—"

"And the Farnham brothers," David cut in, "and their father before them, and their grandfather before that. This was where Jeremy and I spent some of the best years of our lives, though we probably didn't think so at the time."

Diana looked about her with interest. It was indeed a lovely spot, rather like a very prosperous village with a picturesque main street whose quaint shop fronts gave a clue to its age.

"Let's get out for a bit," he said.

"But where is the school itself?" Diana asked as she stepped out of the car and looked around at the fine mansions and high-walled gardens lining the roads.

"We're right in the middle of it. All these are the school 'houses' where the boys live, and that red building over there on the left is Speech Room. This is High Street, and there's the tuck-shop, a very important landmark." He laughed.

"Did you and Jeremy really live here?" Diana asked.

"Yes, of course, for about nine months out of every year when we were in our teens. But not at the same time. I was six years older, you see, but of course we were in the same house. It's along there, just this side of Headmaster's. I'll point it out as we pass."

Suddenly boys were everywhere. They were dressed in dark jackets and trousers, but each had about his neck several swathes of a very long woolen scarf, striped in bright blue and white, and on each head, tipped squarely over the eyes, was a straw "boater."

"Don't you care for the outfits?" David asked, amused when he saw Diana stare at them in surprise.

"The hats! Aren't they a bit odd?" she asked.

"Shsh! That's sacrilege! Boaters are very special hats. Notice how few of them look new. It's the thing to wear your father's old one, or even your grandfather's if it still exists. Noel can have mine if we can't find Jeremy's."

Diana's heart skipped a beat. Oh, no! David couldn't have this in mind for Noel. She felt numb. Surely she was letting her imagination run away with her, and she prayed he hadn't noticed her alarm. *Wait,* she told herself. *Wait. Don't say the wrong thing.* She tried to calm herself as she watched a few men in scholastic gowns and mortarboards approaching. "Masters, I suppose," she said, trying to sound coolly unconcerned.

"Yes, but they're called 'beaks' and they are wearing their 'squares.' Every school has its own jargon, you know." He walked along happily, pointing out what he thought might interest her...the famous playing fields, the library, the chapel, the swimming pool called 'ducker,' the racquets courts, and finally the small statue of Queen Elizabeth I, who had given the school its charter.

"Well, madam," he said at last with mock formality, "have I shown you enough to convince you that this is the right place for your son?"

Diana felt the color ebb from her face. "You're joking."

"Joking?" He swung about in amazement. "Of course not. Where else would he go?"

Diana couldn't believe her ears. Then she looked at him and saw that his astonishment was genuine. She was frightened and bewildered and angry. What right had he to choose

Noel's school? But she made herself relax. There was no need to discuss the matter this very day. She could stave off this conversation until she had recovered from her shock. There was plenty of time, time for so many things to happen. Perhaps she was overreacting. It was just possible that he was simply testing her response.

She tried to laugh. "David, Noel is nine months old."

"I know. That's just the point. Harrovians apply for a place at the school on the day their son is born. I should be getting on with it."

Diana felt her gorge rise. "Do I have to remind you again that Noel had a mother as well as a father?"

"Of course not! But surely this is more my department than yours."

"Why?" she asked, trying to ignore the surge of panic. She had no illusions as to the enormous influence the great British boarding schools had on their pupils. If Noel were taken into one he would be immersed in a whole way of life that she would never be able to maintain. The school fees themselves were far and away beyond her means.

"Diana," David said sternly, "he's a Farnham!"

Diana looked at him coldly. "Is he?" she asked and watched the color fade from David's face. "Noel is also a Verney."

He took a deep breath. "Look, we can't have this discussion in the middle of the road. Let's go in there." They were in front of an old half-timbered tavern, and he grasped her arm and marched her inside.

"What would you like to drink?" he asked coolly, and she could tell by the tautness of his voice that his calm exterior was costing him considerable effort.

"Do I have a choice?" she snapped.

"Oh, don't be a silly girl."

His condescending tone heaped fuel on the flame of her anger. If he was trying to be funny he certainly wasn't succeeding. Without another word he left her and returned shortly with a gin and tonic, which he set before her unceremoniously.

Then, sitting down, he said, "Let's not go back to behaving the way we did when we first met."

"That's not so long ago," she reminded him.

"True, but surely you can see, even in this short time, that my first concern is for Noel."

Diana could, but at the moment it didn't make her feel any easier. "I don't seem to be getting through to you," she insisted. "Noel is *my* responsibility, and *I* intend to support him. Harrow School is quite out of the question."

Irritation flushed his cheeks again. "That's an evasion. When Jeremy was alive you let *him* support Noel. Surely he would have had a say in the boy's education if he had lived."

"That was quite different."

"No, it wasn't. Not all that different. I, too, am a Farnham man trying to care for a Farnham child." David was sounding angrier by the minute. "Noel *is* a Farnham, isn't he? Jeremy *was* his father, wasn't he?"

These new questions made Diana's temper flare again. "How dare you ask such a question?" she cried.

"Oh, I'd dare anything for my brother's son," he assured her, his voice striking at her, toneless and implacable. He stared at her in angry silence for a moment, and then she saw his expression become a fraction less hard. "I apologize for those remarks. I have no doubt about Noel, but surely you can see you are being unreasonable."

Diana shook her head. What she *could* see was that this conversation would lead nowhere. If she'd had a way of getting back to London on her own, she would have left at that moment, but she was stuck and he knew it.

David began again, making an effort to be calm. "Now listen to me, Diana. You know how much a child inherits from his father. Surely you remember the good things Jeremy had to pass on. You couldn't have been as close to him as you were without knowing them. You *must* remember Jeremy's bright mind, his generosity, his basic good nature," David went on. "Surely you hope his son has inherited some of these, don't you? Don't you?" he prodded.

"I—I . . . yes I do," she had to admit.

"Then why can't you accept for Noel something that is of so much less importance? Jeremy never gave much thought to money, probably because he never knew what it was to be really short of it. And he knew, too, that someday he would have quite a lot. Honestly, Diana, I don't see why you won't take a tiny part of his heritage for Noel." He was pale with the effort he was making to put over his point. "What difference does it make that I happen to be holding the purse strings now?"

Diana lowered her head. She knew she sounded foolishly stubborn, but she also knew that every penny she accepted would strengthen the ties between Noel and the Farnhams. She couldn't afford that, but there was no way that she could refute David's arguments. No way, except to admit that she had no right to use anything belonging to Jeremy. Kris would have had that right, of course, but no other woman, and if David were to discover that, she might lose the baby forever.

Then anger took over again. David had no more rights than she had. She and Noel had been doing just fine before he came along. Why couldn't he just leave them alone? The sooner she got rid of David Farnham the better. That was the solution to everything.

"Please take me home now," she said. "If you don't I'll find my own way."

"This argument is nonsensical," David ground out.

"I agree. I thought I had already made it clear that I would not be subsidized by you. I can think of no way to tell you more plainly."

"Oh, I understand you all right," David said, "but I can't believe you understand me. God in heaven, is there no way to make you see that it's Noel I want to do things for, not you? Do you honestly believe you have the right to refuse for him?"

There was that terrible question once again, the question Diana had been asking herself ever since she had met David Farnham. Tears pricked her eyes, and she lifted her head, hoping they wouldn't spill over. "Aren't you taking advantage of—of—"

"Oh, Lord!" he groaned in exasperation. "I didn't mean that the way it sounded. Every mother has the right to say yes or no to anything that has to do with her child. Honestly, I only want to help."

Diana felt a stab of compassion at the note of concern in his voice, and again she was startled by her own reaction. David was becoming dangerous, too dangerous to handle. She must get rid of him, and quickly. She had no other choice.

"Then for heaven's sake," she forced herself to say, "stay out of my life! You weren't invited into it, anyway! Who are you to think you know what's best for Noel?"

Without a word David got to his feet and led the way to the car. They drove back to town in absolute silence, and when they reached her house he hurried around to open the car door for her as if he couldn't get rid of her quickly enough. As she went up the front steps she heard the protest of his tires as he took the corner with uncaring speed.

FOR SEVERAL DAYS Diana turned over and over in her mind what her attitude should be if David were to telephone. She could be "out" a couple of times, but that wouldn't work for long. Every time she remembered his declaration that he would dare anything for his brother's son, she shuddered. She believed him. David Farnham was not to be trifled with.

After a week or two had passed and Diana was becoming reconciled to the fact that David had really gone out of her life, he walked, unannounced, into the boutique. He looked at her coolly without a word and gave Gian-Carlo a man-to-man smile.

"Would it be all right if I take Diana to lunch right now?" he asked.

"No pr-roblem," agreed Gian-Carlo, who had just added the expression to his vocabulary.

"Good! I'll have her back by two."

"Okay. *Buon appetit.*"

Diana was too flabbergasted to say a word. She felt David's strong fingers close around her forearm as he urged her toward the door. She had just enough presence of mind left to snatch up her coat, and in a moment she was in the familiar Jaguar heading for Hyde Park. She glared straight ahead of her, literally too astonished to open her mouth.

He parked the car and turned to her. "Diana, I'm not going to apologize for what I've just done. I knew you wouldn't make a scene in the boutique in front of your boss, and I took advantage of that. We have to talk. I'm sure you know that, too, and I could see no point in wasting time arguing about the necessity of this meeting."

"You may have to talk," Diana said, getting her breath back, "but I have nothing to add to what I told you the last time we met." Nevertheless, she was strangely glad to see him, high-handed tactics or not. Life had been less tense without him, but it had been infinitely less exciting.

"I have nothing to say about that, either," David assured her. "You made yourself quite clear. I need to talk about something quite different."

She looked at him more closely. All the warmth and humor she'd sometimes seen in his face, particularly when he looked at Noel, had disappeared. He returned her look frankly, but there was something new in his eyes that she couldn't read.

"Diana, you and Noel came into my life out of the blue, and your impact was—was more than I realized at first. Then, when we got back from Harrow, I felt that we had come to the end of a relationship that I had misjudged. I felt that you had closed a door and that the best thing I could do for you, and for Noel, was to leave it closed."

Diana had never doubted his sincerity and she spoke as evenly as she could. "Why should that be so difficult? Surely all you have to do is to stay away from us."

"It's not as simple as it sounds," David replied. "You brought something into my life that I can't give up without a fight."

She looked at him aghast. A fight? Was he going to start a lawsuit? She had known from the start that legal action was always a possibility, and that there was no way she could win. She had no money to fight him in the courts or any influential friends to turn to for help. She bit hard on her lip to keep it from trembling.

Suddenly he laid a hand over the fingers she was twisting so tightly in her lap. "Diana, I'm pleading with you."

She looked at him, astonished by the words that he'd delivered so harshly. Had he said "pleading"? David Farnham pleading? Never! "I've really tried to get along with you," she said as smoothly as her unsteady voice would let her.

"I know, and I'm sorry I was so insensitive. Diana, all I'm asking is, couldn't we try again?"

She couldn't help the leap of her heart. The past few weeks had been arid, empty. She had rid herself of the danger this man held for Noel, but with it had gone his big, handsome presence, his breathtaking masculinity.

David was waiting for her answer. His eyes were locked on hers, and again they held that look she didn't quite know what to make of.

Her breath came in small gasps and her words were unsteady. "I suppose I am afraid...that you will take Noel away from me," she ventured, "and I will be left with...with nothing." She had almost said "with neither of you."

"I knew that was your big worry, and I've tried to reassure you but without success. Look, if it will help you, I will introduce you to one of the best legal minds in London. You can talk to him privately, and I'll bet my last penny he will tell you that, as the baby's mother, you would have to do something very nasty indeed to have Noel taken from you."

Diana was shaken. The generosity of his offer undermined her defenses. He *did* mean to play fair, and then anxiety took over again. He had said "the baby's mother." Was that always to trap her? With a real effort she calmed herself. She knew she would have to be very careful.

"David, I believe every word you say. I have never doubted your honesty, but this time you must tell me exactly what it is you would want of me...of us, rather."

"Just the right to see you, to be sure that you don't have to go without at least the simple necessities. I give you my word that I will never again assume that I have the right to do anything more."

Diana's pride rose to help her. "Surely you can see that I'm doing quite well. I have a good job with excellent prospects, a comfortable enough place to live, and help with looking after the baby. What more do I actually need?''

She saw a small spark of anger kindle in his eyes. ''All right, Diana! I agree that you are fine at the moment, but you know I love my brother's son almost as much as you do. I've taken to him in a way that has surprised even me. If you cut me off from him entirely, do you think *I* can live comfortably month after month, year after year, without wondering constantly if he has enough to eat, a roof over his head, warm clothes? All of that, to say nothing of a proper education—'' He broke away quickly from that thought and then continued. ''You must know that life isn't easy for a single parent, yet you'll take no financial help. Can't you see that for my own peace of mind, if for nothing else, I need to be sure that Noel has at least the ordinary necessities of life?'' He paused, then added, ''All I'm asking is that you let me be there in the background, just be there, should you ever be in need of anything.''

Diana turned and faced him squarely. ''David,'' she said soberly, ''I worry about Noel's future too, you know. Often I don't dare let myself wonder what would become of him if anything were to happen to me.'' She swallowed against the tightness in her throat, and searched his face. *Can I really trust him?* she asked herself, and felt the answer come back at her without hesitation. Of course she could. Diana took a quivering breath. ''Maybe we should try again,'' she said.

''Yes. That's all I'm asking,'' he said, and a gusty sigh that seemed to hold relief escaped him. Then she saw the beginning of a smile tug at his lips. ''Lord, but you're an exhausting woman, and my time is up.'' David started the car in a hurry. ''If I'm to stay in Gian-Carlo's good books,'' he said, ''we'll have to make do with a pub lunch. Will that suit you?''

"Of course," Diana answered. She wasn't hungry, but she felt she could certainly use a drink. She remembered someone saying you should drink only when you want to, not when you need to. Little did he know!

"I'd like to see you again on Sunday," he said, as he delivered her to the boutique promptly at two o'clock.

"I would like that, too," she said, "but you would have to include Noel. Mrs. Larkin warned me the other day that she would be too busy to take him for me this weekend."

"No pr-r-roblem!" David said, giving a good Gian-Carlo imitation. "Of course we can manage that."

Diana smiled at the pleasure in his face. "Good. We'll expect you."

She waved to him as the car pulled away, and went back to the jewelry design she had been working on. It looked twice as fine...twice as sparkling as it had before David had practically abducted her.

CHAPTER SIX

"MISS VERNEY, COULD I TALK TO YOU?" Mrs. Larkin asked, surprising Diana since her landlady usually set out for her sister's at the crack of dawn on Sundays.

"Of course. Come on in." Diana was still in her dressing gown, but Noel was dressed and throwing things out of his playpen with his usual abandon. He greeted Mrs. Larkin joyfully.

"Not today, luv." The woman bent over and gave him a hug, and then, with a catch in her voice she said to Diana, "Oh, dear, I hate to tell you this so suddenly, you with a baby and all...but I didn't want to upset you unnecessarily before I knew for sure, either." She paused, distressed, and then went on, "You see," she said, "I'm going to sell this house."

"What!" Diana felt as if the breath had been knocked out of her. Her world was crumbling around her. Had she really heard right? She must have misunderstood. To lose this apartment would be a calamity, but to lose Mrs. Larkin's baby care would be a disaster of the first order.

But the woman was going on. "Remember I told you my sister hadn't been well since she lost her husband? Well, she's going to move to their house in Brighton. They bought it for their retirement, you know, and it has been rented. Now the tenants are moving, and she thinks it would be a good time to take over. She wants me to go with her...and it's the sensible thing for me to do. We could rent rooms to summer visitors and be company for each other the rest of the time."

Diana tried to find words, any words, but it was difficult. She had never considered the possibility of having to leave this inexpensive apartment or Mrs. Larkin's loving child care, at least, not until she was earning more money.

At last she made herself say the right things. "Of course you should go, Mrs. Larkin. Brighton is a lovely place, and you—you get along with your sister..."

"My part of it is all right," the landlady said, "but I worry about my tenants, particularly you. I'll miss the little one."

And how we will miss you, Diana thought. Where would they ever find someone as really kind as this woman. Diana remembered the long and dreary search before she had found Mrs. Larkin in the first place. The thought of going through it all again—

"Well, I'll be on my way, luv." Diana could hear the genuine concern in her voice. "I thought I'd let you know at once. The sooner you start looking for another place the better. They're going to turn this into offices. Can you believe it?" She paused as if searching for a few more words, but finally she shook her head sadly and hurried away.

Diana sat down and stared about her for a long while. She felt like crying. Somehow the thin carpet and the timeworn furniture seemed infinitely desirable. Then the baby gave a wail of frustration, pointing out that he had been too long without attention. Diana picked him up and held him to her. How could she work and look after him at the same time? There were government day-care centers, of course, but she knew nothing about how they were run. Supposing she were to apply for help, would she have to tell them all her circumstances? Supposing they just took Noel away from her—a young woman who wasn't even his mother, with no home and very little money. Could they do that? Could they?

She was back where she had been six months ago, and this time she knew from experience just how dreary the trek ahead of her was going to be. She had a steady job this time, thank goodness, but she knew her salary would fall far short of providing all they would need. Reasonable rents and babies didn't go hand in hand in London, and reliable babysitters were practically nonexistent. Perhaps it would be better if she left London, but that would mean losing her job, and with it her start in the career she had worked so hard to attain.

Noel wailed mournfully and rubbed a flushed cheek against her breast, and Diana hugged him closer. She knew he was teething and that his fretting was normal, but it seemed to bring home to her how little she could do for his comfort.

Suddenly the telephone rang, startling her. Noel refused to be hushed and as she picked up the receiver, she heard David's voice over the baby's wails. "Oh, hello, Diana. I could hardly hear you for a moment. Is that Hotshot making that racket? I hope he's not ill."

"No, nothing to worry about," Diana told him as evenly as she could, trying to match his buoyant tone. "It's just a tooth coming through, and he seems to think it's all my fault, poor little soul."

"You don't sound your usual self, Diana," David said, a hint of worry in his voice. "Are you all right? The baby's not coming down with something, is he?"

"No, honestly, we're both fine," she answered, but at the sound of his friendly voice tears stung her eyes and a lump in her throat threatened to choke her. She had felt so hopelessly alone in the world for the past hour that any sort of friendly gesture would open the floodgates if she wasn't careful.

"You definitely sound under the weather," David insisted.

"No, no, I'm really all right. I just had some unexpected news. Nothing to worry about. Nothing to—"

"Somehow I'm not convinced," he broke in. "I'm going to hang up now, Diana. I'll be there in ten minutes."

Before she could protest, the line went dead. Oh, why couldn't she have hung on to herself a little longer? He was the last person who should find her disheartened.

She hauled on slacks and a sweater, ran a comb through her hair and dragged a lipstick across her pale mouth. That was the best she could do before she heard his car draw up outside. She pressed the door buzzer to let him in.

"David, you didn't need to bother," she said, hoping to reassure him. "I'm perfectly all right."

"So I see. Slightly green around the gills, lipstick smeared, and the buttons of that sweater are out of sync. Call me sometime when you are in trouble. You must be an interesting sight." His banter didn't hide the disquiet in his eyes as he examined her closely. "Aren't you going to ask me to sit down?" he asked.

"Oh, of course. I'm sorry. This is not really something for you to bother about," Diana said.

"Could be you're right," he agreed, "but how about letting me in on it anyway?"

Diana had the feeling that he would keep at her until he was satisfied that he knew exactly what had upset her so, with a shrug of resignation, she repeated Mrs. Larkin's news.

David sat thinking for a minute or two, saying nothing, but she sensed his concern. At last he said, "What we need is to hold a council of war."

Her heart lightened at his "we." It was comforting to have someone worrying along with her.

"I can't stay right at the moment," David went on, getting to his feet, "but can I pick up the two of you later this afternoon? I might have a couple of ideas to offer then."

"I hate to spoil your Sunday," Diana protested.

"Don't give it a thought," he said. "I had nothing special on."

He left at once, and Diana felt happier than she would have thought possible a couple of hours earlier. She felt encouraged by the thought of talking out her problems with David. His support would be heartening.

BY THE MIDDLE OF THE AFTERNOON, Diana was back in David's beautiful drawing room, and Noel had been whisked away by a loving Mrs. Rogers to have his teething problems looked into.

David offered Diana a chair by the fireplace and sat down opposite her, pulling a mock-solemn face.

"Now, as I see it," he began pontifically, "this is a meeting of the 'ways and means' committee. Right?" At her nod he went on, "Let us then take the important issues one by one."

Diana looked at him with amusement, and her confidence was restored. She knew he wasn't entirely joking. Solving problems, after all, was his forte, and she knew he would give this problem, small as it must be to him, the full benefit of his experience.

"Now, as I see it, you need to find a place to live that will house you adequately at a price you can afford, and will offer some care to Noel and let you get to your place of work reasonably easily. Right?"

Again Diana nodded. That was it . . . in a big nutshell.

"Let us talk about your job first since so much depends on it. Are you quite happy with it?" he asked seriously.

"Oh, yes," Diana said quickly. "As I told you before, I'm very lucky to have it. If anything, Gian-Carlo pays me more than I am worth at the moment. Believe me, lots of apprentices would work for him for nothing. What he teaches me is beyond price."

"And you really like him?"

"Of course!" Diana wondered at his persistence. "He's exacting, but fair, and he is a top-class design jeweler."

"No... er... hanky-panky?" David's eyes were more serious than his words.

"Good heavens, no! He's a family man with a wife he dotes on." Diana was flattered in spite of her worries. Obviously this Farnham would take no chances with the welfare of any woman in his life.

"Right." David seemed satisfied. "So the job goes on at all costs."

"Oh, yes." Diana felt at that moment that her work was one of the few sure things in her life.

"Next, then, is to find the place to live, and someone to help with Noel," David went on, "and preferably, the two should go together."

"Yes," Diana agreed, "but that isn't as simple as it sounds."

"Isn't it? Surely they are easily combined, provided you pay enough for them."

"Of course," Diana agreed. "That's pretty obvious."

"And if you don't happen to have enough money, what then?" he probed.

"I just make do with what I *can* afford." Her voice was flat but wary, since she couldn't figure out the direction of his questioning. Yet she felt there *was* a direction.

David was quiet for a moment. "Well," he said, "I could go along with that conclusion if it was only the housing that was involved, but when it comes to the baby, surely we can't just 'make do.' Isn't that a little dangerous?"

Diana's heart sank even further, and she felt as though a weight had settled on her chest. His words were all too true. As far as she herself was concerned, she could get by with very little, but she couldn't take a chance with Noel.

David sat staring into the fire for a few moments, then he turned to her. "Diana, I'm not going to offer you money again. I know it would be a waste of effort, and I can see that at the moment, an argument is the last thing you need. But I can suggest something—and don't turn it down out of hand. At least give it some thought."

Diana braced herself in preparation. "Go ahead," she said slowly, carefully.

"Well, you know a lot of this house isn't being used at present, particularly the old nursery on the top floor. I am offering that to you and Noel until you find something you . . . well, find whatever you want elsewhere."

"But that could be a very long time," Diana managed when she finally got her breath back. "So few places allow children and—and it could be months and months before I can find another apartment."

"I know," he agreed, a gleam coming into his eyes. "That's what I'm counting on. I'm fond of Hotshot, you know. I don't care how long you stay. The longer the better."

Diana looked at him, openmouthed and speechless. He had tossed an idea at her completely out of the blue, an idea that was too big for her to take in all at once. She had seen the rooms he was now offering her on the day she had gone up to the nursery with Mrs. Rogers, and they would solve her problem perfectly. After all, the nursery had been built specifically for children and their nanny, and it was somewhat separate from the rest of the house. But it was under David Farnham's roof. And that was a very big problem.

She looked across at him, sitting calm and relaxed in the firelight. He made no attempt to persuade her but waited, quiet and noncommittal, for her reaction.

"David," she said, grasping at some shreds of common sense, "that's a very generous offer, but—"

"I knew there would be lots of buts," he said. "What's the first one?"

"Simply that there is no way I can make up my mind on the spur of the moment about something so important. I have to think it through first before I can give you any kind of sensible answer."

"Understandable," he agreed. "How long do you think you'll need to work on it?"

"Would a couple of days be all right?"

"Perfect," he said, sounding relieved. "I was afraid you would say after New Year, or some other time in the distant future. It would be much more fun to have you and Noel here for Christmas, you know."

Diana felt her pulse quicken at the thought, and told herself grimly to try to keep a clear head. That was the trouble. His offer was so tempting in so many ways—and as dangerous as an uncharted minefield.

Soon David drove them home, and after he had carried Noel upstairs for her he said, "Diana, I won't deny that I want to have the two of you in my house, but I haven't forgotten what I said to you the other day. I agreed to be in the background in case I'm needed. This way the background will just be a little closer." Then, with a calm, friendly look at her and a soft "Good night, Hotshot" to the baby, he was gone.

For the next two days Diana felt completely at sea, and in a rudderless ship at that. Hopes and fears and memories and conjectures tumbled one over another. It hadn't been easy to keep up the deception about Noel, even when she had seen David only occasionally. Would she really be able to carry it on successfully with much more frequent contact? She told herself that that was her biggest worry, but in her heart of hearts she knew that it was herself she was afraid for. The plain truth was that David Farnham was far too attractive. The memory of those few moments in his arms was still too sweet—it stirred too many longings.

Then she tried to put such thoughts away. To do Noel out of a safe and comfortable home just because she was having trouble coping with her own feelings was ridiculous and unfair, and never would she be unfair to Noel. Never!

When her promised two days were up she went to the telephone and told David she would accept his offer.

"Splendid." The pleasure in his voice was obvious. "I'll come and fetch you so that we can get some details sorted out right away."

"I wish you would. There are some things I hope you will agree to before the move," she said.

In no time his car was at the door. Mrs. Larkin promised to keep an eye on the sleeping Noel, and in no time Diana was back in the now familiar Farnham drawing room. "David, there are a couple of things..." she began hesitantly.

"I knew there would be," he said, greatly overdoing a sigh of resignation. "Let's have them."

"Well, I won't feel right about living here unless I can pay some rent," Diana said. "Could we come to an agreement on that?" She could feel him about to refuse and she hurried on. "Please, David. I know the amount of money I'd be able to pay will mean absolutely nothing to you. It's purely for my own self-respect."

He looked at her for a moment and then nodded. "Right. If that's the way you want it. What about the same amount you paid Mrs. Larkin? Otherwise I'd feel like a profiteer. You know...the heartless landlord who puts the screws on his hapless tenants. Should I grow a mustache so I can twirl it?"

Diana laughed. "I accept," she said, "and I know I'm getting a terrific bargain."

"How about the boy?" David went on. "Your payments to Mrs. Larkin included baby care, didn't they?"

Diana nodded.

"Then, to be fair, that must be provided here, too." She was about to interrupt but he wouldn't let her. "I've already mentioned Polly to you," he went on, "and I've discussed her with Mrs. Rogers. She thinks Polly would be fine for the job."

Diana gasped. Would David always be one jump ahead of her?

"Believe me, you can trust Mrs. R.'s advice," he continued. "She is absolutely delighted with the idea of having a Farnham in the nursery again, and she knows all about children."

"But doesn't she need Polly for other duties?" Diana asked.

"Not really. Polly was engaged a few years ago when— when the house was busier."

Diana saw the twitch of pain and wondered if he had been going to say "When I married."

"To give the job to Polly would be a kindness," he went on. "She adores Noel already, and she lives here, anyway."

"David, how can I thank you?" Diana said simply. There was so much to say, and yet so little.

He disappeared for a moment and then returned, bringing a bottle of champagne in an ice bucket. "Well, for a start, you can help me drink this. It's been ready for an hour. I hoped we would need it to celebrate."

The cork came out of the bottle with a satisfying pop, and Diana held her glass under the sparkling stream.

"Here's to us," David said, "the three of us." They clinked their glasses, and as she saw the pleasure in his face, she hoped she could keep it there at least part of the time.

When the glasses were empty he jumped to his feet. "Let's go upstairs right away and see what needs doing. The nursery hasn't been used for years, you know." For a moment his smile faded, and Diana felt he must be thinking of the baby that might have lived there if his marriage had been different.

He ushered her out of the room and as she turned toward the stairs, he put out a hand to stop her. "Oh, no, you have your own private entrance. Come this way." He took her arm and, leading her into the garden, he hurried her around the house. "Look. There is a door here and it opens onto the back stairs to the nursery. When we were children, Jeremy and I would never have dreamed of coming in any other way. This entrance was ours, and heaven help anyone else who used it. Up you go."

Diana climbed the stairs with delight. This was ideal and when David handed her the keys, she knew he was offering her the privacy she valued.

Although Diana had seen the nursery before, now she was looking at it with different eyes. The big airy children's rooms and the nanny's apartment still looked lived in, if not quite as well kept up as the rest of the house, but that was to be expected since no one had used them for some time.

"It's lovely," Diana sighed happily.

"Yes, it's pleasant enough," David agreed, "but it needs a bit of doing over. I shouldn't have let it go like this. Still, there is one good side to it. Now you can have it decorated the way you would like it. It will make you feel more at home."

"Honestly, David," she said, "I would be perfectly happy with it just as it is."

"No, no, it won't do," he declared. "I should have had the nursery done regularly like the rest of the house. I just haven't been up here in the past few years."

Diana insisted that the rooms were fine just the way they were, but obviously the subject was still on David's mind when they returned to the drawing room.

"I know what to do," he said. "You must have a talk with Molyneaux, the decorator on Sloane Street. He has looked after the rest of this house for years. My mother swears by him. Why don't you go over to the shop and ask him to work out something that would suit you?"

"Well, if you're sure that's what you want," Diana said, excitement welling up inside her, "I'll go tomorrow."

"I insist," he said with a smile. "My new tenants must have nothing but the best. How else can I be sure of keeping them?"

CHAPTER SEVEN

THE NEXT DAY on her lunch break Diana went over to the interior decorator's showroom. Just what she would have expected, she thought, looking around. Rather conventional and obviously very expensive. She didn't hear the approach of the elderly man who greeted her with a formal "Good afternoon, madam," but he was so perfectly suited to his surroundings that she almost laughed aloud.

"Are you Miss Verney by any chance?" he asked, and he smiled when she nodded. "Mr. David Farnham's secretary telephoned to tell us to expect you. We have served the family for three generations," the man went on calmly as he pushed forward a chair for her. "And now, Miss Verney, I understand that you are contemplating decorating a suite in the house for your own use."

Well, that was one way of putting it, Diana thought, and watched with interest Mr. Molyneaux's eyebrows stay precisely where they were. If he had looked amused or even shocked at the idea of a young woman so openly moving in with one of his best customers, she would have understood . . . but his cool formality chilled her. What would he do with the nursery? she wondered. Was she going to end up with an expensively furnished apartment with "a place for everything and everything in its place"? Exactly what she didn't want for Noel.

She watched Mr. Molyneaux purse his lips, look at his well-polished shoe tips and then at the ceiling and back at her again.

"It occurs to me, madam," he said, "that what you need is a decor that will suit the house and yet reflect your youth . . . if you'll excuse my mentioning it."

Diana looked at him more closely. Perhaps she had misjudged him.

"We have a young woman here," he went on, "a junior but very talented. You might find it pleasant to work with her." Diana caught the vestige of a smile on his formal face and smiled back. That sounded much more hopeful.

At that moment, with a click of high-heeled boots and a waft of Guerlain, a girl very like her sister, Kris, in manner blew, rather than walked, into the salon. She had that air of delighted interest that had been part of Kris's particular charm.

"Miss Verney, this is Lavinia Drew."

Diana smiled at the girl, liking her immediately, and was answered by a wholehearted grin that brought the piquant face to life. Lavinia Drew was not strictly beautiful, but dark red hair framed a face so lively and friendly that Diana felt sure few could resist it. Diana would be delighted if this was to be her helper. It would be great fun to have someone like her to talk with.

Diana explained what she needed, and Lavinia was immediately enthusiastic. "I know those houses," she said. "Built around 1800. A lovely period. When may I take a look at your place?"

"As soon as you like," Diana answered.

"Mr. Molyneaux, am I busy?"

"Not as long as Miss Verney needs you, Lavinia," Mr. Molyneaux said and Diana smiled inwardly. Obviously there were advantages to being under the Farnham wing. Well, the sooner they got on with things the better, she thought.

"What about having lunch with me," Diana asked. "I haven't much time, but if there is somewhere nearby that would be reasonably quick . . ."

"There's a super place just around the corner," Lavinia said.

Diana had the feeling that she was going to hear a lot of "supers" in the next few weeks, but it would be marvelous, something to look forward to. She hadn't realized how she had missed having friends like Lavinia to talk to in the past year.

The restaurant was cheerful and crowded, but a place was found for them and soon they were on first-name terms, Lavinia insisting on the less formal Vinnie.

But almost as soon as they were seated, Vinnie looked up from her menu questioningly. "You know, I can't get over the feeling that we've met before somewhere," she said in a puzzled manner. "We haven't, have we?"

Diana forced a smile. "I don't think it's likely," she said. "I've lived most of my life in Oxfordshire."

Diana had known that her resemblance to her sister might raise a question sometime, but as long as David Farnham wasn't nearby surely no harm would be done. Kris's friends weren't likely to overlap with David's, and it was well over a year since any of Kris's photographs had appeared in the press. Still, Vinnie's trained eye might catch what others missed. Diana sighed. It was a chance she would have to take.

To change the subject she pretended to be immersed in the menu, and soon they were enjoying feather-light omelets, followed by truly spectacular fruit salad.

With the coffee they got down to business and when Diana explained her own strict working hours, Lavinia was unconcerned.

"Not to worry," she said. "Decorators are used to working within the client's timetable. It goes with the job, and anyway we'll have Saturdays and Sundays, won't we?"

"Well, yes, but you see..." Diana faltered and then blurted out, "I have a young baby" as she realized how unused she was to explaining Noel to someone she might call friend.

Vinnie took the information completely in her stride. "Just as long as you can keep small fingers out of the paint and paste buckets," she said and shrugged.

"Oh, yes. Noel's too young to really get in the way, but I may have to have him with me now and then," Diana explained.

Vinnie laughed. "Well, it's your place and his home. I'm the intruder. Now, have you thought of getting this done before Christmas? Of course, I don't know what the whole problem is yet, but it doesn't sound too difficult. Nothing structural to change."

"Oh, Vinnie!" Diana's heart leapt. "That would be lovely." It came to her at once how wonderful it would be to have a warm, comfortable, safe place for Noel on his first real Christmas.

Vinnie jumped to her feet the minute lunch was over. It seemed she seldom did anything slowly. "Do you drive?" she asked. When Diana shook her head she said, "Then how about my picking you up when your place closes at five? Gian-Carlo's isn't far from the office. Then we could run over to the house and take a look at what we are up against. If we are to have it ready for Christmas, we'd better get going."

When the workday was over and Diana could finally leave, she found Vinnie already waiting in her smart little car. They drove immediately to the Farnham house, and Vinnie was soon in her element. "This has real possibilities," she told Diana excitedly as she surveyed the nursery. "Thank goodness it's Regency, not Victorian. Now, what colors do you like to live with?"

They were soon immersed in color schemes and hardly heard the knock on the door that connected the nursery with the rest of the house. It was David, and Diana motioned him to come in. "You're my first visitor," she told him. "As you can see, I've wasted no time with the decorating."

"Good! That's what I'd hoped for. Look what I've brought to cheer you on." He handed her a bottle of vintage wine and then smiled at Vinnie. "Don't we know one another?" he asked.

"Um, yes, I think so. Now where... Of course!" Vinnie exclaimed. "The Anstruther wedding. And my brother Peter's bash when he passed his law exams."

"Lavinia Drew," David said, snapping his fingers.

"Right. And you are David Farnham." They shook hands with enthusiasm.

"I told you who my landlord was hours ago," Diana reminded her.

"I know. The name sounded familiar, but now I can put a face to it," Vinnie answered.

Diana was delighted. Somehow the happy chance of Vinnie and David's knowing each other made the whole decorating project seem more friendly and less businesslike.

The three of them spent a fun-filled half hour together. Diana had never seen David looking so genuinely amused before. It gave her an odd feeling to see him so entertained by the vivacious Vinnie, but surely it couldn't be jealousy. Then, as Vinnie was about to leave, David asked, "Have you seen anything of that mad archaeologist lately? Lawford. Wasn't that his name?''

"Not since July," Vinnie answered. "He's in Greece, and he's really not *that* mad." Diana saw a blush creep up to the usually self-possessed Vinnie's earlobes.

"He is, in my book," David declared, a mischievous glint in his eye. "Any chap who is daft enough to leave you alone in London for months..." His rare dimples deepened and so did Vinnie's blush at his teasing. Unaccountably Diana's heart felt lighter. David and Vinnie were friends, she realized, nothing more.

"Diana, can you stay a bit longer?" David asked after she had waved Vinnie goodbye. "There is something I'd like to discuss. I'll drive you home later."

When they were back in the drawing room again David said, "Don't you think it's a waste of time and effort to shuttle back and forth to Mrs. Larkin's while things are being done over here?" He held his hand up when she cleared her throat to answer his question. "Why don't you and Noel just move in now? You can both sleep in the children's bedroom until your own suite is finished, and then you can switch around."

Diana knew the suggestion made sense. She could think of no argument to offer against it, so why was she hesitating? She had agreed to so much already. But it was as if David's generous solution to her problem had been just a dream—and suddenly here was reality. She was being asked to move in *now*—with the baby, and his clothes, and his few small toys—and once she did it, there would be no going back. She would have burned her bridges. For an awful moment she felt panic rise within her. Then common sense reminded her that she had been through all this already and that Noel must remain her principal concern.

"Thank you, David," she said. "I will take you up on that with pleasure."

"Good! Let's ferry Hotshot and his things over right away, and you can move the rest as it suits you."

THAT NIGHT, when Noel was tucked into his cot in the nursery, and she was settling down to sleep for the first time in David Farnham's house, Diana realized how quickly and completely he had taken control of the two of them. It was frightening... and it had all been done so easily. Still, David had promised not to interfere in their lives, and it was comforting to feel so protected.

A couple of nights later, when Diana and Vinnie were hard at work, they heard the now familiar rat-tat-tat at the nursery door. "It's the landlord," David called. "Any problems?"

"David, help us," Diana replied, opening the door to him. "Should we have the wallpaper changed to suit that sofa or have the sofa recovered to suit the wallpaper?"

David shook his head. "After a hard day at the office, what do I get?" He gave a theatrical gesture. "Problems, problems!"

"My heart bleeds for you," Diana said on a laugh, "but we really would be glad of an opinion."

He looked about him, this time more seriously. "You know, you haven't exhausted all the possibilities yet. There are several rooms in the house that aren't used regularly. Why don't you look through them for any furniture that takes your fancy?"

"Oh, David, that's too much. I—I couldn't."

"Objection overruled. It's only a matter of moving a few pieces from one room to another. It will still be my furniture in my house. No pr-roblem, as Gian-Carlo would say. And now that that's settled, would you mind if I just take a look at Hotshot? Life is a lot more peaceful around him than it is with you two these days.''

''He's probably asleep,'' Diana warned, and then watched him make for the playroom with painstaking stealth.

''We'd better not get started on a furniture search to-night,'' Vinnie said when David had gone. ''I'll be around bright and early tomorrow morning.''

The next day was Saturday and when Vinnie arrived, David had already gone out, leaving a message for them to carry on without him. They'd found one or two pieces that would suit Diana's apartment beautifully, when Vinnie asked, ''Did we look in here?'' As she threw open a door she whistled in surprise. ''What a gorgeous set of rooms, but why on earth are they empty? This must be the loveliest suite in the house. And look at that wall covering. Imported silk damask.''

Diana looked around. There was a sitting room, bedroom, and bathroom, beautifully proportioned and with a splendid view. And they had been stripped. There were no coverings on the floors, even the fixtures had been ripped out of the bathroom. It was then that they came upon the locked door, and Diana realized that it must lead to David's own quarters. There was a devastation about the empty rooms that chilled her, as if everything had been ripped out in despairing grief or terrible anger.

Even Vinnie seemed subdued when they went back to the nursery. ''Makes you almost want to ask where they have hidden the body, doesn't it?'' she said.

Diana nodded her head and then turned to her companion. ''Vinnie...you and David have been friends.... Do you know anything about his ex-wife?'' she asked.

''Not really. Only that my brothers seem to think that David was well rid of her. By the look of those rooms, he must have thought so, too. I know her slightly,'' Vinnie went on. "She's sort of on the edges of our crowd, but she's never been a friend of mine. She's done quite a bit of modeling—has the looks for it, certainly. But she only models for kicks, not the money. The woman's loaded. Have you met her?"

"No, I've only known David for a couple of months—"

"What?" Vinnie was staring at her, openmouthed.

"Oh, dear," Diana sighed. "I should have told you. I simply forgot that you would likely think that David is Noel's father. No, he's the baby's uncle. Noel is Jeremy Farnham's son."

"I see," Vinnie said. She still looked slightly bewildered, but she was far too considerate to press for further explanations.

Diana was so tired of having to tread warily around the truth that she would have liked to tell Vinnie the whole story, but it was safer to change the subject.

"WE'LL BE THROUGH HERE this week," Vinnie said a few days later. "It's good, isn't it?" she coaxed, looking around with satisfaction.

"Perfect," Diana agreed, reveling in the clear, cool colors picked up from the fine Aubusson carpet they had found in a seldom-used guest room.

"Couldn't be better," David said when they sought his approval, "but shouldn't you be having some sort of party to celebrate the end of all this hard work? A nursery warming, or something?"

Diana said nothing. She realized how really few friends she had in London and how long it had been since she had gone to a party of any kind. There was a moment of stillness, and she knew that David had caught her mood.

"I have an idea you might go for," he said. "You know there is a supper dance at the Dorchester next Saturday."

"Yes," Vinnie said. "The big charity do for Children's Aid."

"I bought a table months ago," David went on, "although I didn't really expect to use it. Suppose we have a party there."

"Super!" Vinnie cried. "Oh, Diana, I know they are having a couple of really good bands."

"Is the mad archaeologist back?" David asked, and grinned when Vinnie nodded. "And how about your brother and—look, can I leave it to you two, please? I know it's a bit late. I should have thought of it sooner."

"Don't worry, David," Vinnie assured him. "Just leave it to us."

When he had left she looked at Diana, eyebrows raised. "You don't look exactly delighted about this party," she said. "Did I jump in too soon as usual? I'm sorry if I did."

"No, no. It's just that, well, won't it be very dressy? It's ages since I last wore an evening gown. I know it sounds an awful cliché, but honestly I haven't a thing to wear."

"Surely we can get around that," Vinnie said. "Let's see. My things won't fit you, but—wait! I have an idea." She went off to make a telephone call and came back beaming.

"It's fixed. Didi Lansborough will lend you a dress."

"Lansborough? You're joking. Her stuff is gorgeous. I think she is the best of the younger designers. How on earth did you manage that?" Diana gasped.

"Oh . . . I promised you would design the jewelry for her next collection. I told her you were Gian-Carlo's favorite assistant, and his terrific reputation did the rest."

"But that's fabulous. It will be marvelous for the jewelry, too. Great publicity. Thanks." Diana hugged her.

"Yes, I'm wonderful, aren't I?" Vinnie agreed with an exaggerated lack of modesty.

With a sponsor like Vinnie, Didi Lansborough and her staff accepted Diana as one of themselves, and the next afternoon Diana was standing in bra and panties being impersonally looked over by the owner of the salon, two assistants, a fitter and Vinnie. Diana was amused at the wholehearted way they threw themselves into finding just the right dress, but they were professionals and they knew their job.

"Now, let's see. If the princess is to be there, that means lots of slipper satin and bugle beads. The dowagers will be out in force," one of the assistants said.

"Right. Upholstered bosoms and tiaras," the fitter added.

"Wall-to-wall sequins—"

"Oh, look here," Vinnie broke in, "she can't look as if she just came off the top of the Christmas tree."

"No, no, leave it to us," Didi said. "If Diana is to make an impact, she will have to go in for sweet simplicity. With her looks and coloring, naive and fragile is the right approach."

"What about the white organza?"

Diana let them argue among themselves, content to wait until they produced a few dresses for her to try on. Some time later she agreed with their choice. When she put on the organza she knew it was the one. Its bodice, below her bared shoulders, was demure at first glance, but the delicate material was sheer enough to hint excitingly at what lay beneath, and the myriad of tiny pleats in the softly tiered skirt shimmered like butterfly wings at her slightest move. The dress would be a dream to dance in.

"Cor!" exclaimed Vinnie. "David had better bring his dueling pistols."

"Now, be sure to sweep your hair up," Didi advised. "No girlish curls. We want youthful sophistication, not Little Bo-peep."

Diana giggled, and went home in high spirits.

"All set for Saturday then?" David asked the next day.

"Oh, yes. Vinnie is bringing Bill Lawford, her mad archaeologist, and both her brothers will be there with their girls."

"Good. You'll like them. They're a cheerful lot. I haven't seen them since...for quite some time." The hesitation was noticeable, but it passed in a second. "Then I'll pick you up at nine o'clock." He gave her a teasing grin. "Your place or mine?"

"Yours." She smiled back.

"Right, then. The front hall. Handy, this arrangement, isn't it?"

Diana was looking forward to the party with real excitement. There would be so many firsts...her first formal dance in London, her first beautiful evening gown in ages, her first meeting with a circle of new friends—and, above all, her first big date with David.

She hugged herself with delight as she went to bed. Tomorrow would be a night to remember. But just before she dropped off to sleep, another thought broke through. Was she getting in too deep? No, she wouldn't think about that now....

CHAPTER EIGHT

A SURGE OF DELIGHTED EXPECTANCY swept Diana toward her date with David on Saturday night. She laughed happily at her own excitement; she hadn't felt like this since her first high school prom. It had been a long time since she'd had a formal date with a handsome man, she told herself, and a long time since she had dressed for one, too.

But she was unworried, for she knew that tonight she looked her best. The gossamer dress shimmered and shifted against her body with her every breath. The warm ivory of her shoulders lifted above the provocative bodice of golden embroidery, which matched the sheen of her high-piled hair. Delicate earrings glinted at her ears and shot blue fire to echo the sparkle in her eyes.

She hesitated for a moment at the top of the stairs and looked down to where David stood adjusting his cuffs. She was used to his impressive looks by now, but she had never before seen him in full evening dress.

The stark black and white etched his frame with precision and seemed to make his shoulders broader, his waist leaner, his long thighs more muscular. With his thick hair brushed to perfect order and jeweled studs winking from his shirtfront and cuffs, he might have walked straight out of a romance novel.

With a shiver of pleasure Diana started down to meet him. As he lifted his head to look up at her, astonishment held him in utter stillness for a moment. Only his eyes moved, following her as she came toward him. For a second she wondered how it would feel to keep on walking until she met with the thrilling resistance of that wide, strong chest. She stopped, and for a moment there seemed to be no one in the world but the two of them.

The deep-pile carpet soft beneath their feet, the gentle gleam from the damask walls, the whisper of tinkling sound from the crystal chandelier, the intimate scent of David's subtle after-shave—all seemed to wrap the two of them in a sensuous cocoon. Then he stepped toward her, moistening his lips as if they had suddenly become dry.

"Will I do?" she asked, breaking the spell.

The broad smile she had seen so seldom broke across his face. "Would you care to rephrase that, Diana?" he asked, pretending to mop a fevered brow. "I'm only flesh and blood, you know." Then, laughing, he offered her his arm. "You look absolutely fabulous, Miss Verney," he said. "Now let's go to the ball."

For Diana the car ride was a blur of excitement. As she took off her wrap in the cloakroom of the Dorchester, always impressive, but now gay with Christmas finery, she heard a familiar "Super!" and turned to meet Vinnie's inspection and triumphant smile.

"The dress is absolutely bang on, isn't it? Does David like it? But how could he help but like it?" Vinnie was in her usual high spirits, answering her own questions almost before she had finished asking them. "My brothers are here and so is Bill. They are at the table already. See you shortly."

Diana was anxious to join the others, but first she was to go with David to be presented to the dance's royal patron. They made the required bow and curtsy and when the princess acknowledged them graciously, Diana realized it wasn't at all the formidable experience she had feared.

David smiled down at her and gave her an encouraging wink as he offered her his arm at the ballroom door. She felt a thrill of pleasure at the rustle of interest caused by their entrance, and knew that she was with one of the most eligible men in London. David, too, had noticed the small flurry, and made no attempt to conceal a satisfied grin as he led her to their table. "Ah-ha!" he said, bending to whisper in her ear, "my men friends are green with envy already."

"David, stop smirking," she scolded. "I'm sure you have been to hundreds of dances like this."

"Of course I have, but tonight I'm with the most beautiful girl in the place. Why shouldn't I be smug? There isn't another woman in sight who can compare with you."

Surprised by the sudden compliment Diana looked up into his face, sure that she would find some sign of his teasing, but she saw only sincerity. She quickly turned away from him as if to admire the great room made beautiful by myriads of flowers and shaded lights, but really her action was to conceal the tremor of guilt that had brushed her with cold fingers. Was it fair to David to be here among his friends when she knew she hadn't been completely honest with him? Was she letting herself become too involved, she wondered, too involved for his sake a well as her own? But she had seldom seen him look so carefree. Perhaps this once... As if from far away she felt gentle pressure upon her shoulders. He was waiting for her answer to a question she hadn't even heard.

"You're neglecting me already," he said with a mock frown. "I asked you if you liked dancing."

"Yes, I—I do. I haven't danced for a long time, but I love it," she said, and shivered at the thought of his arms around her.

"That's lucky," he said, "for I have a feeling that every chap I have ever even nodded to in the past is going to remember suddenly that we are longtime buddies."

And he was right. A great many men did seem to know David, but he good-naturedly waved them aside. "The first dance with my beautiful partner is mine," he said, "and the second and the third and the fourth, and after that who knows?"

She smiled at him. This was no time to go back to her problems. The best thing she could do was to make this evening as happy as possible.

For a moment he looked down at her with a strangely serious gaze, and then as his arms closed around her she felt with compelling certainty that, at last, she was where she belonged. His grip tightened and as her hand slipped up around his shoulder, he bent his head toward her, and the warmth of his breath fanned her cheek.

She should have known he would dance well, she thought, and she gave herself up to the rhythm of his strong body as he moved to the music. She was able to follow his steps with ease, and she smiled inwardly as she felt him begin to try her out with some fancier movements. Both she and Kris had always danced well, and Diana knew she could keep up with anything David might try. Soon she could sense his pleasure in her expertise, which matched his own, and she felt grateful when he refused to relinquish her to other partners.

After a while the orchestra left the podium to take a break and was replaced by a far less formal pop group. The discreet lighting gave way to theatrical flashes of swirling color, and Diana watched as David's fingers tapped out the beat on the tabletop. He noticed her amusement and, without a word, lifted his eyebrows and nodded toward the dance floor. The fact that they'd just sat down hardly mattered.

As they danced, she began to feel an increase in the sensuousness of the rhythm. David was gazing across at her with an intensity that seemed to challenge her, and she felt herself submit without resistance to his dominance. As the movements of her body answered his, his mouth softened into a smile, and the distance between them decreased until just one small move of his head would bring his lips down on hers in a kiss of...of...what? As the music stopped, she pulled herself away with a sudden jolt of awareness. For a fleeting moment she had seen the hunger on his face, a hunger that she had understood.

As they walked back to the table, Diana's head was spinning. She wondered if it was the music or the wine or just the nearness of David that was tearing at her defenses. Whatever it was, she warned herself to be careful. The situation had reached a dangerous temperature.

Then she suddenly asked herself, *Couldn't I simply enjoy myself this once? And enjoy David too?* It was the first time she had seen him looking as young as his thirty-two years. Surely, she reasoned, there could be no harm in just enjoying the party. After all, a dance floor was a very public place, and who was to know, except herself, what the feel of his arms did to her?

Then the bands were changing around again, and the lights were softening, and everyone danced with everyone. Diana wasn't short of partners, and David enjoyed an occasional dance with Vinnie and the other girls at his table. The evening was going well until...

David was leaning back, relaxed, watching the others, when suddenly Diana saw him stiffen. She followed his glare as a spectacularly beautiful woman came toward them. A green gown that shouted Paris from every seam caressed her superb figure, and thick black hair cascaded over one shoulder. A fabulous emerald necklace echoed the green of exotically tilted eyes that were measuring David with amusement.

"Why, David," the woman murmured deep in her throat, "how lovely to see you after all this time."

"Good evening, Marcia," David said formally as he got to his feet.

"Oh, indeed it is." The woman's tone was taunting. "And you are looking particularly well."

As the green eyes turned to take her in, Diana was supremely thankful for the beautiful Lansborough gown she was wearing. It, at least, could stand up to any examination.

"Aren't you going to introduce us, David?" the woman asked.

David's face was impassive, and his voice was toneless as he spoke. "Diana, this is Marcia Beresford. Marcia—Miss Verney."

Marcia acknowledged Diana with a careless nod, almost with an air of dismissal. "You won't mind my borrowing David for this dance, will you? We haven't seen one another for ages."

Diana looked at the white line around David's mouth— and sudden anger shook her. Why should this woman spoil David's evening? He had been so relaxed and happy. Then the orchestra started to play the unmistakable opening bars of the "Blue Danube." Diana spoke in a tinkling voice she didn't know she possessed. "Oh, I'm afraid I can't give him up just at the moment, Miss Beresford. I've been looking forward to a Viennese waltz all evening. Perhaps later..." She smiled innocently at Marcia Beresford and, placing a firm hand on David's sleeve, she steered him toward the dance floor.

Diana heard a muffled splutter of laughter from Vinnie's direction, and she took a quick glance at David's face. A muscle was jumping in his tightly clenched jaw but as the music swept over them, she felt him begin to relax.

"David," she ventured. "I hope I didn't do the wrong thing. I got the idea that that woman was upsetting you."

David shrugged. "It wouldn't be the first time. That woman is my ex-wife," he said simply.

Diana missed a step. "Oh, I'm sorry. I—I had no idea who she was."

"Don't be sorry," he said, his voice as firm as his expression. "My days of dancing to Marcia's tune are long since past."

Diana looked around when David led her from the dance floor, and she saw the green dress draped over a willing shirtfront, but Marcia didn't come back to their table. Through the rest of the evening Diana watched David carry on like the good host he was, but the pleasure seemed to have left his face. The thought began to gnaw at the back of her mind that perhaps it still hurt him to see Marcia in another man's arms, and it was obvious that David was relieved when the party finally broke up.

When they got to the house he offered her a nightcap, and when she refused it, he didn't try to change her mind. She thanked him for the party and went up to her apartment, wishing desperately that she could have taken away the bleak look from his eyes.

Diana went to bed but sleep wouldn't come. She tossed and turned for what seemed hours until finally she got up to look for a book. But she couldn't settle down to read either... and then she remembered the drink David had offered her before they had said good-night. Perhaps she should have taken it, she thought. Wasn't that what people did when they were upset? Poured themselves a drink? She was feeling exasperated enough to try anything. She had no liquor in her apartment, but she knew she was welcome to help herself from the drawing room's drinks table.

She slipped on a negligee and crept down the stairs. There was a reflected light so she could see her way, and she caught the flicker of firelight through the partly open drawing-room door. Good, she thought, the fire was still burning. Perhaps if she sat beside it for a while her nerves would untie themselves and she would finally get some sleep. At least it was worth a try, and she went over to the table to pour her drink.

"Pour me one, too."

Diana jumped at the quiet voice and nearly dropped the decanter. She turned quickly to see David slumped on the sofa. She hadn't noticed him in the soft light, but she drew a deep breath and asked as steadily as she could, "What will you have?"

"Scotch and water, please—and make it a double."

She did as he asked and took the glass to him and when she had poured a smaller one for herself, she looked at him more closely. She didn't think he was drunk, but obviously he'd had a few drinks since they came home. He still wore his black dress trousers, but his coat and tie were off, and his white shirt was open to the waist. A lock of hair clung rakishly to his sweat-damp forehead, and she saw the pulse beating strongly in his neck. Her own heartbeat quickened as her eyes slid downward to the enticing shadow of the dark hair on his chest. She could smell the masculine aura of him and she felt the tip of her tongue slide involuntarily along her lips as if it had tasted a forbidden fruit.

"Sit here," he said, patting the sofa beside him. "I promise not to eat you."

David's mocking undertone worried her, but she sat where he indicated.

He clinked his glass against hers and said bitterly, "Here's to beautiful women," and tossed back his drink in one gulp.

"And handsome men—" She tried to match his mood and almost managed to imitate him, but her gesture went wrong at the last minute and ended in a choking, tear-streaming splutter.

"Let that be a lesson to you," David laughed, pounding her on the back and taking the drink from her hand. Then the teasing light in his eyes changed. "That outfit you have on is even more attractive than the one you wore to the dance," he said, as he leaned forward to examine the pale lavender chiffon negligee that had belonged to her sister, Kris. The matching nightdress underneath was even less substantial than the top layer, and Diana was thankful that the light was low.

"But you haven't taken your hair down yet," he went on. "I think I like it best hanging loose. Here. Let me do it."

Before she realized what he intended to do, he had set down his glass and was carefully removing her hairpins. She shivered at the touch of his fingers and the warm palms that burned against her temples as he freed the shimmering waves.

"There. I think that's better."

She looked deep into his eyes, which were so close to her own, and reality faded. The whole great city seemed asleep around them. In the quiet room with its soft golden light, its flickering fire and the scent of flowers, the sound of his breathing was as intimate as a caress until she felt it quicken. Suddenly she realized that the man beside her was no longer the David Farnham she thought she knew. The cool mask had slipped, and she saw with breath-quickening excitement the hot-blooded demand that lay beneath.

His lips were only inches from her own, and she felt him shudder as they came nearer. Suddenly, as if giving up a struggle, a great groan broke from him. He thrust his arms around her and pulled her to him. Her eyes closed at the first touch of his lips against hers, and she lay in his arms. Willingly she gave him the sweetness he demanded, and moved her head to offer him everything he craved. She slipped her hands up behind his head to crush his kiss against her own, and he drank from her like a thirsty man in a desert. She trembled against him as she felt his kissing exploration at the hollows of her neck . . . then around to tease her ear.

Then David lifted her like a child and laid her along the length of the wide sofa. She reached for him, savoring every touch of him. As he slipped the nightdress from her shoulders, without thinking, she arched to offer her breasts to his questing mouth. His lips enticed and teased her until she thought she could bear no more. This was no storybook lovemaking; this was the imperious demand for fulfillment of a hungry and passionate man. Her pulse raced as she felt his breath come deeper and faster, and then she bore the bliss of his weight upon her. She moved against the surge of his masculine desire, felt the need to answer its compelling rhythm. But when he impatiently tossed aside his shirt— suddenly Diana was jolted into frightening awareness.

She saw with awful clarity that she was teetering on the brink of disaster. If she let David take her now, at the very moment of fulfillment, at the peak of his need for her, he would know that she had lied to him, know that she had never belonged to any man. He would know she could not have been Noel's—any child's—mother. She could not, *must* not, let him go on. Feeling hysteria mounting, she pushed him away. There was no time to explain. No time for words of any kind.

For a moment she felt his resistance as he tried to overcome her own. "Diana—you can't leave me now. You must . . . you must . . ."

His words tore into her despairing heart, so that as she thrust herself from his grasp she felt his agony...and her own body echoed it.

She heard no call as she fled upstairs. She threw herself on her bed in the dark and crawled under the covers as if to hide from what she had done. For a long time she lay there shivering with hopeless despair—and longing.

Every fiber of her ached to run back to David's arms.

DIANA AWOKE from a fitful sleep to a gray and bleak morning. The very idea of breakfast appalled her, and she made a large pot of coffee, instead. She thought the strong brew might give her a bit of a lift, but she wasn't really hopeful. It would take a lot more than coffee to drag her out of the clammy swamp of despair that was slowly engulfing her.

How could she have been so mindless, so insensitive, so unfeeling, as to let David go so far last night? Let him? She could feel a hot blush scald her face. She knew she had done considerably more than "let him" as she remembered her response to his eager arms, his hungry mouth. And yet even now her breath caught on a stab of desire when she remembered the longing he'd aroused in her. The very thought of seeing him again made her skin hot with embarrassment. Yet the thought of not seeing him was even more painful.

She was pouring herself another cup of scalding coffee when Vinnie telephoned to ask if she could drop by to collect some magazines she had left behind. Diana said yes eagerly, for Vinnie's presence and the sound of her cheerful voice would be a help.

"Cor!" Vinnie exclaimed when she arrived. "What's eating you? Last night you were the belle of the ball, but this morning... That must be the hangover to end all hangovers."

"No, nothing like that," Diana said, wishing it were that simple. "Sometimes I...well, I do and say silly things...."

"So what's new about that? Don't we all? Welcome to the club." Vinnie sounded unconcerned, but Diana caught her looking at her with speculative eyes. Diana poured her guest a cup of coffee and went off for the magazines in an effort to stop this dangerous conversation from going any further.

"This what you want?" she asked, dropping the magazines on the table.

Vinnie leafed through one of them idly as she sipped her coffee. "Yes, I'm looking for something I saw a while back that— Good heavens!" She stared at Diana wide-eyed and then back at the magazine. "I've never seen such a resemblance."

Diana peered down at the full-page spread Vinnie held out. It was Kris. She was standing sideways to the camera, a Paris gown showing off her lovely figure. Her head was turned to the photographer, a smile curving her lips, and a glance of mischievous invitation lit her dark eyes. Diana fought to hold back her tears, but a sob escaped her. The likeness had caught not only Kris's beauty but her sweet-tempered gaiety, as well.

"Diana, dear, what's the matter?" Vinnie asked, dropping the magazine and reaching out to her.

Diana could hold back her sobs no longer. Her nerves were already in tatters, and this was the last straw. She had to confide in someone, someone with a warm heart and a willing ear. Above all, someone she could trust. "That's my sister." She managed to choke the words out.

"I'm not surprised," Vinnie said gently. "You are so alike and—my word, isn't she a beauty?"

"Was," Diana whispered. "She has been dead nearly a year."

"Oh, no!" Vinnie took up the magazine again and stared at the picture, shock written on her face. "What an awful shame. Do you want to tell me about it?"

Diana looked into Vinnie's kind eyes. "Oh, Vinnie," she sobbed, "you don't know how much I need to tell somebody." She felt her whole body begin to shake. Somehow, now that she had the chance to talk, her strength was melting away. Vinnie brought her a glass of water, and it rattled against her teeth as she tried to drink. She managed a sip or two and gradually felt her control return.

"Vinnie, please listen to what I have to tell you, but first, promise," she begged, "promise you will never breathe a word of it to anyone."

"Of course," Vinnie answered instantly. "I promise."

Diana drew in a deep breath. "It started well over a year ago..." she began, and then went on with the whole sad story, sparing herself nothing, leaving nothing out. As she talked she watched her friend's face for signs of disapproval, but she found only compassion and sympathy.

"Oh, you poor thing!" Vinnie said when Diana had finished. "What an awful load you've been carrying around. But you have to stop blaming yourself. As far as I can see, you have always put your sister's baby first over everything."

"Yes, I think that's true," Diana agreed, "and in the beginning it all seemed so simple. I thought my only concern was to keep my promise to my sister. I knew that it meant hard work, but I was willing to take that on. Just having the baby was a tremendous reward."

"I can understand that," Vinnie said. "He's a super little chap. He has everybody twisted around his finger."

"Yes," Diana agreed, "particularly David. You see, at first I had no idea of just how much the Farnhams had to offer Noel. Oh, I knew they had plenty of money, but it never occurred to me to worry about all the other things. If Jeremy had lived, it might have been different—Jeremy might have had other children—but Noel is now the only grandchild, the only Farnham of his generation.''

One of Vinnie's eyebrows lifted. ''And how long do you think that's going to last?'' she asked. ''I've never seen a man who looked more capable of sorting out that kind of problem than David Farnham. He'll have children...lots of them someday.''

Diana was silent. The secrets of David's marriage weren't hers to tell. Besides, in spite of all its present turmoil, her heart still felt a pang at the thought of David marrying again, holding his wife in his arms, taking her to his bed...looking forward to the birth of his child. She shook her head hopelessly. That sort of thinking could only add to her misery.

Vinnie sat deep in thought, her elbows on the table and her chin in her hands. Then she directed questioning eyes at Diana. ''You've really thought this deception through then?'' she asked.

''Lord, yes,'' Diana answered. ''I've tossed and turned ideas until they are all frayed at the edges.''

''Then Noel really presents a double-edged problem. He will lose too much if you keep him from the Farnhams, and you will lose too much if they take him away from you.''

''Yes, that's it,'' Diana agreed, and wondered why Vinnie was looking at her so intently, and why the shadow of a smile was lifting her friend's mouth.

''You know, I don't think you are laying it all on the line.'' Vinnie went on. ''There's a third angle, isn't there?''

''A third?''

''Oh, yes. And isn't it your biggest worry?''

Diana looked at Vinnie seriously, almost afraid to let her go on. ''Which is?'' she whispered finally.

"You are worried to pieces about how David Farnham will react when he hears the whole story, what he will do when the dust clears. You know how he feels about Noel, how he feels for his family, but how he will go on feeling about you is the big question, isn't it?" Vinnie broke off. "I'm right, aren't I?" she insisted. "David really matters to you, too."

Diana gazed at Vinnie wordlessly. Had she been that transparent? She hadn't really admitted to herself yet how really afraid she was of losing David, that he was as dear to her as the baby, as dear to her as her dead sister, as dear to her as anything in the whole world.

She saw Vinnie's smile deepen. "Stop worrying yourself to a frazzle," she said. "Certainly you have many things to tell David, but you're a big girl now. Surely you know by this time that a man in love will forgive anything."

Diana jumped. "What did you say?"

"I said a man in love will—oh, come on now," Vinnie teased. "Give me credit for having eyes in my head. Of course the man's in love with you."

"If only I could believe that," Diana breathed.

"Believe it." Vinnie nodded vigorously. She glanced at her watch and jumped to her feet. "Look, I've got to run, but a last word of advice. Tell David.... Tell him soon, and tell him yourself. It would be a disaster if he found out any other way."

When Vinnie had gone, Diana sat for a long time staring into space. Was it possible that David did love her? Were those eager arms and those passionate kisses last night really for her and not just the impulsive acts of a virile man greedy to be consoled by the nearest woman? Her pulse quickened at the memory of his lovemaking, but even so her thoughts faltered. If Vinnie was right and David was in love, wouldn't it be with the selfless, devoted young mother he thought she was? Would his love survive if he knew she was really a fraud?

Diana felt her mind going around in circles again, and she was tired of worrying, of trying to sort out her problems. But she knew Vinnie had been right about one thing....

She must tell David the truth.

And soon.

IT WAS NEARLY NINE O'CLOCK that evening when she heard David's knock at her door. She had heard nothing from him all that day, and he hadn't made his usual Sunday visit to Noel, so she was acutely ill at ease when she opened the door to him.

His eyes burned dark in his pale face. "May I come in?" he asked. She motioned him to a chair, but he remained standing. "Diana, there is no way I can live with myself until I tell you how sorry I am about last night. I—"

"David, please," she broke in, her heart twisting at his flat, pain-filled voice, "I'm sorry about last night, too." She couldn't let him take all the blame if she could help him. "It was such a lovely evening," she ventured, "and—and—"

"Yes, until I brought it crashing about our ears." His tone was bitter. "I promised you, when I persuaded you to come here, that you would have nothing like that to worry about. You, my own brother's—"

"Don't say it." She almost sobbed. "Please, please, David—don't!" Diana was so anxious to stop him that she knew she was on the verge of blurting out the whole truth. But she knew that, while it had to be told, this wasn't the right time. If what Vinnie thought was true, she must find a way to tell him that would give him the least pain. It would be no pleasure to any man to find that the woman he loved had been lying to him.

Diana forced a smile to her stiff lips. "David," she said, "I know last night wasn't what either of us intended it to be. Can't you see that I am human too, and need allowances made for me, as well?" She thought she saw his tension ease a little, and she went on. "Why must you blame only yourself? Don't you remember, I was the one who came downstairs uninvited? I poured myself a drink? I was the one who turned up with practically nothing on?" She saw a slight flicker of emotion cross his face. Anything was better, she thought, than the frozen mask he had worn when he first came in. "Don't you understand that my conscience won't give me any peace unless you let me take at least part of the blame?" With relief she saw his expression soften.

"Diana, I would be grateful if you would just forget the whole thing." Then he added, "Even though I know that's a lot to ask."

"Oh, it is," she said, smiling at last. "Far too much. I don't want to forget all of it. Please, let me hold on to the glamorous bits. That was the loveliest party I'd ever been to in my whole life."

The smile he gave her was still strained, but at least it was a smile. "And you were the most beautiful partner I ever took to one," he said. For a moment he looked deep into her eyes. Then he lifted her hand to his lips, kissed it gently and quickly turned and left the apartment.

Suddenly her sitting room looked bright and cozy again, and she sat there for a long time. Her heart felt much quieter. Tonight she would sleep, she knew, and tomorrow, when she felt refreshed, she would think through the complications that lay ahead. For the first time she felt the stirring of hope that she might find a way to tell David the truth without losing him forever.

CHAPTER NINE

THE SHOP WAS UNUSUALLY BUSY for a Monday. It seemed to have dawned on the customers over the weekend that Christmas would be upon them soon. Diana noticed that Gian-Carlo's romantic soul was torn between delight at the special things his clients wanted for their ladies and exasperation at having a stream of last-minute orders. Diana was swept into the general excitement and was kept so busy that personal matters had to be shelved for the time being. There was no opportunity today to work quietly while she sorted through her problems. Still, she thought, it might be a blessing in disguise. If she were to get away from her troubles for a little while, she might see them more clearly, more objectively, later.

When she left the shop that evening, however, she realized that she had just been indulging in a little wishful thinking. As her difficulties came crowding back in on her, Diana could see that there would be no easy solution. Her most urgent problem still was to find the right time to talk to David. It was not simply a question of the quicker the better.

Christmas was now only a scant two weeks away, and the whole Farnham household was gearing up for the festivities. Mrs. Rogers was icing fruitcakes that she'd baked months earlier, an enormous turkey was hanging in the larder, and Rogers was cursing gently as he picked roasted chestnuts from their shells.

"Never mind him," Mrs. Rogers said comfortably as Diana looked into the big, cheery kitchen. "I sometimes think he would rather eat chestnut stuffing than the turkey itself, so he might as well work for it."

Everyone seemed to be caught up in holiday preparations. Anna was at a side table briskly polishing a huge silver punch bowl, and Polly was holding up a small pair of bright red mittens she was finishing for Noel.

"I think they look a bit big, madam," she said anxiously.

"Well, nothing wrong with that," Diana soothed. "They might do for next winter as well."

Next winter? Would Noel still be here next winter? But more to the point, Diana wondered if *she* would still be here with him. As she turned away from the bright kitchen with all its warmth and mouth-watering scents, she knew she must not take the baby out of this happy security. *No matter what might happen to her, Noel must stay here.*

She went slowly upstairs. Was it only a year since Kris had died bringing Noel into the world? So much had happened in those twelve months, more than in the rest of her whole life, and the most devastating happening had been the advent of David Farnham. And he had had his share of miserable Christmases too, she remembered, as she glanced into the nursery at the sleeping baby. She wanted, above everything now, to get this crushing load of guilt off her shoulders, but did she have to spoil this Christmas for David as well? Again Vinnie's warning "Tell him soon!" rang through her mind, and again she probed every possibility. At long last, almost despairing, she settled on the day after Christmas for her confession. The thought of delaying terrified her, but it was the earliest date she could choose and not risk ruining Christmas.

To her surprise, Diana felt her spirits lighten almost at once. She had lived for so long with this guilt clouding her existence that the thought of getting rid of it, no matter what the cost, was a great relief.

Just what the cost would be she had no way of knowing. It was beyond her to predict what David's reaction would be to her story. He might never want to set eyes on her again, despite Vinnie's assurance that he loved her. Love, Diana suspected, could be killed off all too easily by deceit. But one thing she was sure of: Nothing would kill David's love for Noel. And another thing: No one had the right, not even on the strength of a deathbed promise, to deprive Noel of all that David's love could do for him. He could give Noel so much more than she ever could, things such as a privileged background, an excellent education, a career boost, even an honored name.

And if David should want her, too, then, quite simply, all would be right with the world.

DIANA HAD A DATE to have lunch with Vinnie the next day, and resolved to reveal the deadline she had set for herself. It would make the plan more definite, she thought, more like burning her bridges. When she had told Vinnie, there could be no retreat.

Vinnie whisked her away from the shop at top speed as usual. "I want you to see this restaurant," she said. "I have just finished redoing the decor, and the management wants to step up the publicity. I think you'll like it." When they were settled at a table Vinnie looked at her keenly. "You look a bit less fraught today. Are things going better?"

Diana nodded and explained what she intended to do.

"Well, no one can blame you for wanting to keep things on an even keel until after Christmas," Vinnie said, "but be careful, won't you? You are walking a tightrope and al-

though you've been doing it for quite a while, that doesn't
make it any safer."

"Oh, I'll be careful," Diana assured her. "I'm just relieved that the end of all this is in sight, no matter how it
turns out."

"Ladies—look this way, please." They looked up and for
a moment were blinded by a camera flash. "Thanks." A
cheerful young photographer waved.

"What was that for, James?" Vinnie called to him.

Trust Vinnie to know everyone, Diana thought.

"I'm doing a spread for the restaurant's new publicity,"
the young man answered, coming over to their table. "Glad
you dropped in, Vin. Photogenic ladies are just what the
doctor ordered."

"Flattery will get you everywhere." Vinnie laughed, and
he was about to move away when he swung back, and it was
precisely at that moment that Diana experienced an odd,
sinking feeling.

"Diana? It can't be you," he said excitedly, and Diana
winced. "Marvelous to see you again. I didn't recognize you
at first. It must be a year since we last met...and you're
certainly blooming. You're just as beautiful now as...as..."
He stopped in confusion.

Diana knew he had been about to say "as your sister,"
and she shook her head. "No," she said, "no one will ever
be quite like Kris."

"That's true," the young man agreed. "We all still miss
her, you know."

Diana was glad when Vinnie interrupted to ask about the
flash photos. "Oh, these are for the advertising agency," the
photographer explained, and Diana's heart sank. What if
some reference was made to her as Kris's sister? And what
if David saw them before she had a chance to explain?

"Stop worrying," Vinnie said later. "So you had a sister. You even had a pregnant sister. What does that prove?"

Soon Vinnie took off in her usual jet-propelled style, and Diana resolved to take to heart her warnings about being careful. For the next couple of weeks she would watch every step, weigh every word.

She ran into David that evening and was glad to see him looking less tense. "Are you planning anything special for Christmas?" she asked.

"Not officially," he answered, "but it has been a tradition since before I was born to have open house here on Christmas afternoon. Everyone we know is welcome and we are never really sure who will turn up."

"Are your parents likely to be back?"

"I doubt it. As far as I know my father hasn't told mother about Noel yet. He's sure she'll want to come back the minute she hears about her grandson, and my father is still worried about her health. He thinks it would be better for her to finish their cruise. He's bound to be dying to see the boy but for now he has to concentrate on what's best for Mother."

Diana was relieved. She had agreed to let David tell his father about Noel some time ago, but now that she had made up her mind to tell David everything, she wanted to avoid added complications until she got her confession over with.

"Well, if you need any help with your Christmas party just let me know," she offered.

"Good. You're on, then." He was immediately enthusiastic. "A beautiful hostess will liven things up no end. Mrs. Rogers will give you the lowdown."

Mrs. Rogers seemed pleased when Diana went to talk with her. "There hasn't been a really big crowd here for a long time," she said. "But with you here, madam, we might get

back to normal. I hope so. There was nothing Mr. David
used to enjoy more than having his friends in.''

That evening they set up a large Christmas tree in the
curve of the staircase. Everyone seemed to be involved, from
Rogers's filling a great tub with earth to Polly's dribbling
silver icicles on every twig she could reach. When David at
last put the hall lights off and the tree lights on, it looked like
a lovely Christmas card.

Diana gazed at the tree with delight, and then for a moment sadness filled her as her thoughts went back to the
previous Christmas.

David must have caught the shadow on her face for he
said suddenly, ''Speaking of lights, Diana, have you ever
seen the famous Regent Street decorations? I imagine you
were a bit too busy last year.'' As Diana shook her head, he
said, ''Good. Come on, let's go now. I'll get Rogers to drop
us off since parking space will be at a premium tonight.''

Diana had hardly time to draw a breath before she was
stepping out of the Daimler at Piccadilly Circus, and then
she gasped in sheer wonderment at what she saw. The great,
classic curve of Regent Street was festooned from end to end
with ropes and garlands of colored lights, and exotic fruits
and flowers of spun glass dangled enticingly above the slow-
moving traffic. Every shop's doorway beckoned like an entrance to Aladdin's cave, and Diana felt a childlike excitement as she stepped forward to see farther around the bend.

''Careful. Don't step in the gutter.'' David's strong arm
closed on hers and held her warm and safe until she had
gazed her fill.

''It's magical, David,'' she gasped, and she could see by
his smile that he was delighted to be showing her this won-
derland for the first time.

"The Regent Street lights always were the beginning of Christmas for Jeremy and me," he told her. "I hope I've started you, too, on that tradition."

Diana wondered for a moment just what she would be doing this time next year, but David's mood was infectious, and her spirits lifted again.

Suddenly he stopped walking. "Do you think we could do a little bit of shopping?" he asked. "I was going to give the household staff cheques this year since my mother isn't here to help me pick gifts, but it seems awfully cold-blooded. What do you think? Could we manage to select some things, even if it is the last minute?"

"Oh, that would be fun," she said and laughed. "Surely you know by this time that there's nothing a woman likes better than spending money." She was rewarded by the broad smile she loved, dimples and all, and they made their way up toward Oxford Street.

Diana spent a blissful hour or two looking for just the right things, and David bought whatever she suggested, despite his assurance that he would never be able to present the frillier items himself. Diana laughed at the idea that he would be shy of anything, and had more than a little difficulty keeping him from buying her everything she looked at twice.

"No, no, David," she insisted. "You don't have to buy me anything. Some women love just looking, you know."

"So do men," he assured her with a grin, and his eyes, resting on her flushed cheeks, left her in no doubt as to where he, at least, was looking. Then he glanced at his watch. "Let's go over to Soho for a nightcap," he said. "We should be able to make it just before closing time."

The narrow streets seemed dark after the brilliance of Regent Street, but they soon turned into an ancient pub, bright with Christmas decorations and the blaze of a great

log in the fireplace. It was crowded, but David found Diana
a seat just as the landlord called "Last orders, please."

"Just made it," David said and went to the bar.

As he left her, Diana's heart jumped. Not again, she
thought. At a far table she saw James, the man who had
photographed her and Vinnie in the restaurant. He was with
a group of young men—and most of them looked familiar
to her. Diana felt almost sick as her fears came pushing
back, and she prayed that she wouldn't be noticed. But that
was too much to hope for. At that moment James caught
sight of her, and he smiled with pleasure and started coming toward her.

"Diana," he called, "here you are again. Always seems
to go like that, doesn't it? You don't see someone for ages,
and then you run into them two or three times in the same
week. Mind you," he went on, "I'm not complaining." He
nodded toward his table. "Like to join us? I think you have
met all that lot."

"No, thanks, James," she said, grateful that the lineup
at the bar was detaining David. "I'm with someone."

"Bring him along, too. The more the merrier."

"Well, actually I think he would rather be just with
me . . ." she said, squirming inwardly at deliberately sounding so coy.

"Can't say I blame him," James said, and, after giving
her an understanding grin, he went back to his friends. He
must have said a word or two to them about her, for they all
turned and waved. Diana was just waving back when David
arrived with their drinks.

"Friends of yours?" he asked and when she nodded, he
continued, "Sorry I can't buy them a drink. The landlord
has just called 'time.' "

"Oh, I imagine they've had plenty," she said, trying to
look unconcerned. She drew another breath of relief as the

throng at the other table began to break up, but her respite was short-lived. James paused as he passed their table.

"Diana, why don't you drop in for my New Year's party?" he said. "I'm in the same place, and it would be great to have you back. Just like old times. Remember how Kris could keep a party going...?" He went on with a few more words, but Diana was too agitated to really hear them. All she wanted was to stop him from saying more.

"Oh...er, thank you, James," she said, hurrying her words. "I'll do my best. I'll give you a ring."

Then James was swept away by his friends, and Diana breathed again. She couldn't remember exactly what James had said, but she didn't think any damage had been done. If David sensed anything was wrong, he made no comment as they finished their drinks.

When they got home Diana thanked him for the lovely evening.

"I enjoyed it, too," he replied with a smile. "There's a lot to be said for 'just looking.'" Then he added, "Why don't you ask those friends you met in the pub to drop in here on Christmas Day? I'm sorry, I should have thought of it sooner. This should be open house for your friends, too, you know."

"Oh, but that's not necessary," she protested. "You have already invited Gian-Carlo and his wife, and Vinnie and her brothers." The last thing Diana wanted was to see any more of her former acquaintances. Not until after Christmas, until after she had explained to David.

But David seemed unwilling to let the matter drop. "I insist. I feel guilty about not thinking of your friends earlier. Please go ahead and invite them. James and his crowd seemed a pleasant lot, and I've no doubt that any one of them could keep a party going."

Diana was startled. He was referring to James's comment about Kris. And when she thought of it, she realized how lucky she'd been that James hadn't said anything else about her sister. Her nerves were still jangling. Her escape from disaster had been too narrow to pass it off lightly. Then David said a cheerful good-night and she hurried up to her apartment, happy for once to be leaving him.

When she reached her bedroom she heaved a deep sigh. Just one false word in the pub and her world would have come tumbling down about her ears. So much had hung on the slim thread of chance.

But would that thread hold long enough?

AT BREAKFAST THE NEXT MORNING Diana mulled over the events of the previous evening. The morning light seemed to give her a better perspective, and she put away her nerves of the night before and thought instead about the fun she'd had. She was smiling over David's present-buying spree when it occurred to her that it would be nice if Noel could give David a present, too. She was giving him a set of very new records that she knew he would like, but what could she find for Noel to give? She thought about it all the way to the boutique but hadn't the glimmer of an idea.

"The trouble is," she complained to Vinnie later, "the man has everything."

"I couldn't agree with you more," Vinnie said, giggling, "and I can think of at least a dozen women who would go along with that."

"Big help you are," Diana grumbled, and went on to tell Vinnie about her close call of the night before. Probably it was talking about Noel and the young photographer in practically the same breath that sparked off the idea of giving David a photograph of the baby for Christmas.

"I'm sure he would like it," she told Vinnie, "and I could make a silver frame for it myself. That would be no trouble for me, and there is always a good supply of silver in the workroom. But I'm wondering if I've left it too late to book a photographer."

"Maybe not," said Vinnie. "The photography itself doesn't take all that long. It's all the malarkey about appointments and sittings and that sort of thing that takes the time. Leave it to me. I have my contacts."

Vinnie was as good as her word. The very next day Diana took Rogers into her confidence, and she and Noel were whisked off in the limousine to the studio where Vinnie had arranged an appointment.

"I stayed away from the purely fashion photographers," Vinnie had explained, "just in case one should recognize you. John Barrington goes in mostly for stage work, so you should be all right with him."

Diana was a shade worried. The photographer's name had a familiar ring, but there was no time to pick and choose. However, when she reached the studio, she knew her worst fears had been justified. Barrington looked at her with astonishment. "Diana," he cried, "how lovely to see you again, my dear. When Vinnie asked me to do a hurry-up job for a friend, I had no idea it was for Kris's sister. She said Miss Verney, and I didn't associate the name with Kris. After all, she was—was always just dear Kris to all of us."

Diana could see that he was deeply moved by the memories she'd surprised in him, and she hurried on to explain that it was Kris's baby who was to be his photo subject.

"My dear, we were all shattered at what happened to Kris," he went on, and Diana was touched by the warm sympathy written on his face when he looked at the little boy.

"What a charmer!" Barrington said. "Babies are not generally my cup of tea, but this one is a bit special, isn't he? And of course he has Kris's eyes. Unmistakable. I will do something beautiful with him, just wait and see."

When she saw the photographs a day or so later, Diana had to admit that they were indeed exceptional. The baby was looking out at the world expecting to be loved. The soft little mouth was curved in a beguiling smile, but by a clever use of light, a hint of wistfulness seemed to linger at the back of the velvet-brown eyes. It was a minor masterpiece.

But the worry about knowing Barrington stayed with her. "I suppose it was to be expected," Vinnie said when Diana phoned her. "If he asks me any questions I will just play everything down. After all, it's perfectly natural for you to be looking after your sister's child."

"But Barrington has my address in care of David Farnham," she pointed out.

Vinnie gave a chuckle. "If this situation weren't a bit dangerous at the moment, it would be funny. First you were an unwed mother, and now you are an unbedded girl-friend."

"Very funny," Diana retorted, but Vinnie's joking had taken a little bit of the edge off her nerves, which was probably what Vinnie had intended to do. "Barrington just took one look at Noel and knew who he was," she said.

"Well, it's no world-shaking story," Vinnie commented. "These photographers all seem to know one another, but you're not planning to keep the details from David for much longer, anyway, and he's the only person that counts now."

"So you really can't think of anyone who might give things away?" Diana asked.

"No, not with Marcia Beresford out of David's life. She dabbled a bit in modeling, of course, so she may still know that crowd, but why should she bother to talk about Noel with anyone? She has no way of knowing that there is a connection or that you have anything to hide." Vinnie paused, and Diana could almost visualize her encouraging smile. "Just hang in there. And think how marvelous it will be to have all this behind you."

Diana crossed her fingers for luck and couldn't make up her mind whether she wished that December 26 would come in a hurry, or stay away for a very long time.

CHAPTER TEN

DAVID WAS GETTING OUT OF HIS CAR as Diana reached home that evening. "Look what I've got," he said, holding out a flat package, a well-known record shop's name across it. "If you're free tonight, come downstairs and hear them with me."

"Thank you, I'd love to. What did you get?"

"Some Christmas music for the party and more Domingo for you. What's he got that I haven't got, anyway?" he said, grinning.

"Well, a wonderful voice, for one thing...and I'm not sure what you'd look like in tights." Diana laughed.

"Why, I'd look magnificent," he said, giving her a glower of mock reproof.

He probably would, too, Diana thought as she went up to her apartment. She wasn't really sure whether she should join David later or not. Perhaps it would be better to keep her distance now that she had made up her mind to admit the truth. She remembered how, early on, she had thought how comforting it would be to have David Farnham for a friend, just that and nothing more. She should have had the good sense to keep things that way. To let herself feel anything deeper for a man like David was asking for trouble, and she should have known it. Still, he had obviously set his heart on making this a good Christmas for everybody. She should at least try to meet him halfway.

When she entered the drawing room later, he motioned
her to the sofa, but she almost jumped up again when she
remembered the last time they had sat there together on the
night of the dance. Then, telling herself not to be so silly, she
settled back to listen to the music.

David had changed from his city clothes and was
stretched out comfortably in an armchair on the opposite
side of the fireplace. The tranquil music filled the room,
seeming to heighten the gentle glow from the fire.

David had closed his eyes, so she could let her gaze wan-
der freely over him without danger of getting caught. The
wayward lock of dark hair had fallen onto his forehead, as
usual, and the music had soothed his strong face into unaccustomed vulnerability. He looked younger, more sensi-
tive, more understanding. Was this the real David or—?
Then she remembered the photograph of him laughing with
his brother Jeremy that she had seen upstairs. It was as if,
after that, he had built a wall to protect himself from further hurt.

The top buttons of his silk shirt were undone and there
were small curls of hair on his chest just visible at his neckline. She felt hot blood mount to her cheeks as she remembered the feel of the hard muscles under his velvet skin.
Suddenly his eyes opened, and she was gazing into the gray-
black depths that seemed to be saying something she dared
not comprehend. For a timeless moment his eyes bound her
and then released her.

When the music ended David seemed to shake himself
free from the spell that had held them both and stepped
across to change the record.

Diana waited, but no sound came to break the stillness.
She looked at him, surprised, but he was standing quite
motionless, his back to her and his head bowed as if he were
in deep thought.

Suddenly he swung around. "Diana, I have to talk to you." Her heart missed a beat. A sudden change of mood like this wasn't his usual style. She watched as he strode over to stand where she had so often seen him, in front of the fireplace, with one arm along the mantelpiece, his head bent to look into the flames. She wondered why he was having so much difficulty saying what was on his mind...and a flicker of fear stirred within her.

"I hadn't intended to say this to you tonight. I know I should put it off, but I have to get it over with. But where to start..."

Diana shuddered. It wasn't like him to be hesitant. Had it to do with Noel, or her living in his house, or his parents, or—? Every possibility seemed to hold some sort of menace for her.

"Oh, heaven help me!" The cry that burst from him was of sheer exasperation. In a single stride he was standing over her, his hands closing on her shoulders as if he meant to shake her, his eyes blazing down into hers. "Diana, I need you. I need you in my heart as well as in my house."

Diana's heart nearly leapt out of her body. She stared at him, unbelieving. "David, I—I—" Suddenly she was on her feet, almost ready to run from him.

"I can understand your astonishment," he said, the shadow of a wry smile appearing. "Believe me, so am I. But there's no way I can go on like this. I need you, and I must have you. If there is no chance for me, then the sooner I learn to live with that the better. I've never known how to handle uncertainty, and when it involves you..."

His arms reached for her and in them there was no uncertainty—only hunger. For a long moment he held her against the heavy thud of his heart, and she knew he was going to kiss her before his lips neared her own. They closed on hers, gently at first . . . and then with an urgency that left her breathless.

Joy flooded her. Oh, David, David! her heart cried out to him, and then came the cold clutch of fear. What he was offering her was for that other girl, the one he thought he knew, the one who had mothered his brother's child and who now held a place in his family—not her at all.

He looked at her tenderly. "You know, the other night I thought you felt as I did. I could feel all your sweetness answering me. Tell me . . . tell me it wasn't all fantasy."

She looked into his face and tried to step away from him. "David, there are so many things you don't know," she said.

"Of course there are," he agreed, "and one of these days I'll listen to everything you want to tell me, but right this minute all I want is for you to tell me that someday you could love me."

"But we've never talked very much about the past—about Jeremy or—"

"Believe me, I'm not trying to push Jeremy out of your life, Diana. I loved him too, you know. I only want to know if you could one day find a place in your heart for me, as well."

"You know practically nothing about me," she said, her voice rising in pitch, "about other people in my life, about—"

"Shh." A warm finger stopped her lips. "You are not really listening. This is between us, you and me. Jeremy, Noel, my family, our friends—none of them matter. This is about *us* and *our* future. There is no room for anything else just now. Don't you see that?"

She turned away from him, close to tears. "Oh, why won't you listen?" she entreated.

142   LOVE'S PERJURY

Suddenly she was in his arms again, her words cut off by his demanding mouth. She could fight no longer. She gave her lips to his, to the burning sweetness she loved so well.

At last he lifted his head and said, "That's why I won't listen to your words." His arms loosened a little and then folded her to him more gently, and she felt again the pressure of his muscular thighs and the stirring of his hunger.

Panic seized her. She must stop him while she still could. There had been times in the past when she had turned away from men who had wanted her. But she hadn't wanted them, and had always felt the need to save herself for the man she would one day truly love. Now, when she had found that man, it was ironic that she must turn from him in order to hide the fact that she had been with no man before him.

"Please... David, please!"

His arms fell away from her and although he was breathing painfully fast, he made no further attempt to touch her. But he held his ground and she could still sense the urgency of his desire. His whole being seemed to be telling her of his need for her, but it was a need for much, much more than physical satisfaction. There had been infinitely more than passion in his long, sweet kiss.

"Diana, can you honestly tell me that kiss was all on my side?" he asked harshly. "I think it told me all I need to know for now. Didn't it?" He slipped a finger under her chin and tilted her face to look into her eyes. "Didn't it?" he insisted.

She couldn't lie to him. "Yes," she whispered, "but it doesn't change the fact that—that you don't know the real me."

"Maybe not," he said, "but the one I know will do well enough for now. There can't be *that* much difference."

Diana felt battered. How simple it might have been if she had just been honest with him in the first place. Or would he have bothered with her at all, then? More likely he would have taken Noel from her and left her to get on with her life—alone.

His declaration of love had been overwhelming, but it had changed nothing for her. He still didn't know the truth; he still believed her to be something she was not. If only she could tell him the truth now... but her lie had been too big. It couldn't be tossed off with a forgiving smile. She needed a few days' grace—and there was Christmas for the whole household to think of, as well. If she spoiled it for David, everyone would suffer. No—she must stick to her deadline.

"David, I'm sorry I can't—can't..." Her voice trailed off as she saw tiny beads of sweat on his forehead.

"Go on..." he said.

"I—I can't answer you right this minute. Please don't ask me to. Could you possibly wait a few days to talk about this? It was...rather unexpected."

His sigh filled the room. "You'll be the death of me yet," he complained. "Do you think you could give me some idea of how long I am to totter on the brink of a nervous breakdown?"

Diana looked up into his handsome face, so controlled and closed once again. She gathered together all her fortitude and ventured, "Would the day after Christmas be all right?"

"It's better than seven years, with time off for good behavior. I can't pretend to have a clue to what's holding you back, but, then, it would take a braver man than I to say he understands women. Just make sure that when you answer me, you answer me honestly."

Then suddenly he saw that the conversation had exhausted Diana, and he hurried to make amends. "I should have noticed sooner how tired you are. I should have sent you to bed long ago. Come." And before she knew what he was about, he had picked her up to carry her to her apartment. He lifted her into his arms effortlessly and when she protested that she was too heavy, he paid no attention. A teasing light came back into his eyes, and his steps grew slower and slower. At last, when they finally reached her door, he seemed reluctant to set her back on her feet again. Still he held her close.

"I think I should warn you," he said, "that I intend to do everything I can think of to 'woo and win you' in the few days you have left to me. No holds barred."

Then he bent and kissed her on the lips and left her.

DIANA HAD EXPECTED to toss and turn in bed as she had done so often lately, but the memory of David's "I need you" had soothed her troubled spirit, and she had gone to sleep with her cheek resting upon a pillow that, in the night, had somehow changed into his broad shoulder. And the next morning, Diana felt completely rested.

This was to be her last day at the boutique until after the New Year. She dressed in a simple shirtwaist in her favorite shade of soft blue, brushed her hair until it shone golden about her shoulders, and pulled it back with a matching Alice band. Then she heard David at the door.

"You look far too young to be courted by anyone outside of high school," he said when she opened the door.

"'Courted'? Goodness. Is that what you have in mind?" she asked.

"Don't you ever doubt it, lady," he said, skimming her cheek with a freshly-shaven chin. "You may only have given me a couple of days, but I intend to make the most of them."

The fresh tang of his after-shave teased her senses for a moment, but he made no further move toward her. "Aren't you going to open that before you have your breakfast?" he asked, nodding toward an enormous florists' box propped outside her door.

"For me?" she gasped.

"Well, I'm pretty sure it's not for Noel." David grinned as he moved the box inside for her.

Diana undid the ribbon with care, and lifted the lid. The box was brimming with the most lush, long-stemmed, deep-red roses she had ever seen.

"Oh, David, how beautiful. How on earth did you get them delivered at this time in the morning?"

"Actually, I didn't. I went to the flower market myself." He laughed at her wide-eyed stare. "It's quite a while since I was anybody's boyfriend, but I remember roughly how it's done."

He certainly did. In the course of the morning a flat box of exquisite chocolates arrived at the boutique from Bond Street, and was soon followed by a messenger from a famous bookshop bearing half a dozen of the month's best-sellers. Then, in the middle of the afternoon, David telephoned.

"If you're not busy tonight, may I take you out? I can probably borrow my father's car."

Diana laughed. "Can you wait until I look at my date book?"

"If I must...but mind you," he warned, "the girls usually snap me up."

Diana thought there was probably a great deal of truth in that. He must have been pretty devastating at seventeen or eighteen. Still was, for that matter, she admitted wryly. "What did you have in mind?" she asked.

"Dinner at L'Écu de France and then the Royal Philharmonic at the Albert Hall."

"That sounds heavenly, but isn't it a gala performance? Can you get seats at such short notice?"

"Don't worry about that. I've already got them."

Diana shrugged. She should have remembered that he had a habit of getting what he wanted. "That would be wonderful," she said. "It's been a long time since I've listened to a live orchestra."

"Me, too. Well, can I pick you up about seven?"

"Yes. I'll be waiting on the stairs."

She chose for the evening a black chiffon cocktail dress that Vinnie had talked her into buying at Didi's. She knew the black would do nice things for the cream of her skin and the gleam of her hair.

"I call it my Fallen Angel dress," Didi had said as she tossed it over a chair back. It had looked fairly ordinary lying there but once Diana had it on she could see what Didi meant. The simple overdress could almost have been demure, with its long sleeves and modest neckline. Almost, that is, if it hadn't been cut from chiffon that was as sheer as a gentle mist, and was draped over a strapless, figure-hugging foundation. It was a dress that advertised nothing, but caught the eye by the luscious mysteries it only hinted at.

Diana had a slow, scented bath and smoothed her skin with fragrant body lotion. As she ran her hands over her uptilted breasts, she brushed the buds of the nipples and remembered how they had risen against much larger and harder palms. She saw in the steamy mirror the warm blush stain her cheeks. Had the thought of those provocative minutes with David come back to excite her—or to warn her?

She brushed her hair and then pinned it high again. She slipped into black panties, drew on gossamer stockings and stepped into the dress. It did everything for her that she had hoped it would. Then she put on high-heeled sandals, gave herself a last scan in the mirror, and began tiptoeing softly down the stairs to wait for David.

She peeked over the banister as he stepped out of the drawing room to check his wristwatch against the grandfather clock in the hall. He was wearing formal dinner clothes, and the uncompromising black and white was relieved by a deep blue cummerbund and a ruffle on his shirtfront that added a dash of romance.

As the last chime of seven o'clock died away, Diana gave an affected little cough and tried to look as if she had been waiting for hours.

"We did say seven o'clock, didn't we?" she asked. "And your mouth is open."

He was staring at her, a glint of desire in his eyes. "I'm not surprised," he finally said. "You look good enough to eat. You know, that dress isn't fair to defenseless men."

"You'll live—and you're hardly defenseless." She laughed, and they left the house in high spirits.

The French restaurant was everything she could have expected, although they didn't have time to linger over coffee. The Albert Hall was filled when they arrived, but they reached their seats in a grand-tier box in plenty of time.

The great circular auditorium was Victorian splendor at its most lush, from the organ's massive golden pipes to the velvet draperies on the boxes. The audience's expectant murmur quieted as the orchestra took its place, and then the conductor strode to the podium with a no-nonsense briskness. That was the last commonplace moment Diana remembered. The rest was sheer magic.

The world-famous orchestra responded with enthusiasm to its dynamic director, and from the first bars of the opening Mozart to the closing strains of the last encore, it wrapped the audience in magnificent sound. David hardly said a word to her. He didn't need to; the music said it all. Once or twice she looked at him and found him gazing at her with such unconcealed tenderness that her heart seemed

to melt, and when the great heartrending melodies of a
Tchaikovsky symphony churned through her blood, he
picked up her hand and held it in both of his against the
thud of his heart.

When the concert finally ended and they were leaving the
hall, he asked, "Would you like to do something else?
Dance at the Savoy, maybe? It's not terribly late."

"Oh, no. Who could listen to any other music after what
we have just heard? Let's just go home."

"Let's go home," he repeated. "Sounds good, doesn't
it?" And his arm tightened around her as they walked to the
car.

When they were back in the drawing room, he offered her
a nightcap, as usual, and she took her place by the fire while
he poured the brandy. He handed her a glass and then sat
down on the hearth rug near her. She moved her knee to give
him a comfortable backrest, and for a long time they sat,
quietly watching the flames and sipping the golden cognac.

Diana relaxed in the gentle silence, enjoying the memory
of the superb music she had just listened to, and savoring the
nearness of the man she loved. When at last she said a soft
good-night, he walked her to her door and gave her a gentle
kiss.

It had all been so right, so peaceful. But how much more
blissful it would have been, she thought, to have walked the
few steps to his door rather than to hers.

IT WAS NOEL'S BIRTHDAY, and she went in to see the baby
first thing in the morning, but David was there before her.
She found the two of them flat on their stomachs on the
nursery floor playing some kind of complicated game with
small, colored cars. She wasn't quite sure how much the
baby could contribute to the game but they were both ab-
sorbed in it.

"Happy birthday, darling," she cried, dropping on her knees to kiss the little face raised up to her own.

"Favoritism," David growled, giving Noel an eyeball-to-eyeball glower, but Noel merely gurgled with pleasure and threw his arms around David's head.

A sob caught in Diana's throat as she watched their playful wrestling match. David should get married and have a son of his own, she thought. Then he would never have to learn that Diana had deceived him.

But now he had declared his desire for her, a desire that might never find fulfillment, and she knew that as long as she remained the love of his life, he would never look at another woman.

The love of his life? Her heart wept, for he was the love of her life, too.

CHAPTER ELEVEN

WHEN DIANA AWOKE, she looked out the window with delight on the Christmas morning. It had snowed heavily in the night and big, clinging snowflakes were still falling, holding softly to the tree branches and spreading a carpet of pristine white. She switched on the radio as she dressed and every station seemed to be "jingling bells" with abandon. She pulled on a Christmassy-looking pair of red slacks and a soft white sweater and tied her hair back with a bright green and red ribbon. Good! With a spot of lipstick she would do, she thought, and lifted her chin determinedly. This was to be a happy day, she insisted, as she pushed aside a faint clutch of anxiety and went across the hall to the nursery.

David was steadying Noel, who was standing on the window seat, his little starfish hands spread on the glass as if trying to catch the falling flakes. When Diana stepped closer, David put his free arm around her, and for a minute the three of them stood in one embrace, and the sheer happiness that shone from David's face made her heart melt.

Then Polly bustled in with Noel's breakfast, and Diana offered David some coffee before they went down to the Christmas tree.

As usual, David seemed to overwhelm her small kitchen, and she felt her pulses quicken as she looked at him. Immaculate white flannels hugged his long legs, a heavy white silk shirt was folded comfortably back from his forearms, and a brightly patterned ascot made a splash of color at his neck. The white threw into contrast the healthy glow of his skin and the deep gray of his eyes as he looked at her steadily from beneath almost black brows.

"You're beautiful," he said quietly.

And that's just what I think of you, she mused, but it was hardly the sort of thing to say to a great chunk of virility like David Farnham.

"Just a minute," he said. "I have a finishing touch." He disappeared but was back in a moment with a sprig of mistletoe, which he fastened in her hair with gentle fingers.

"Won't you need that yourself?" she said.

"No, not as long as it's with you. Still, you might pay a little something for it. Look. No hands…" And he held his hands shoulder high as he bent toward her.

She looked into his honest eyes and at his gentle mouth. Then she stood on her toes and kissed him, long and firmly, on the lips.

He stood back, his breath coming fast. "You do take your life in your hands sometimes, don't you?" But his deep dimples showed how much he had enjoyed her rashness.

When they went downstairs to the Christmas tree, David entered wholeheartedly into the fun of being Father Christmas. The pile of gifts beside the tree had grown considerably since the night before, and there was a joyous hour of "oohs" and "ahs" and rustling tissue paper and scattered ribbons. The things Diana had helped David buy for the staff were a great success, and everybody, down to Mrs. Rogers's pampered cat, had something for Noel.

Then Diana held a small package in her hands. When she opened it, she almost dropped it. There, on a bed of velvet, lay one of the most beautiful sapphire bracelets she had ever seen. She recognized immediately the master touch of its

maker, and suddenly she remembered David and Gian-
Carlo in a number of quiet huddles in the past several weeks.

"David!" she gasped. "You can't give me anything as
valuable as this."

"Who, me? Read the card, my love," he instructed.
"That's from Noel. Ever try arguing with a baby?" David
turned away and pretended to be unable to hear anything
further in the general melee. It was the most gorgeous present Diana had ever had in her entire life, but was it just one
more part of her that she would have to leave behind when
she told David the truth?

Noel's photograph, in its elegant, simple frame, was the
success of the morning. After trying it in various places,
David decided that the middle of the drawing room mantelpiece was the best place to show it off. "I may want it in my
study, later," he said, "but that's definitely its place, at least
for Christmas."

Diana felt that the photograph was a bit conspicuous
there, but she was delighted that David was so pleased with
it. After all, it was his Christmas present. He could put it
anywhere he liked.

She had a late lunch with David, and then they both took
Noel for a run in the snow in his new red sled. Afterward she
had no trouble in sending both David and Noel up for a nap,
and then she lay down for a rest herself before getting ready
for the party. There was no telling how many guests would
turn up, and she wanted to be at her best.

At half past four Diana put on the cocktail dress she had
worn to the concert, and added the beautiful bracelet David had given her. She might never wear it again, but she had
to enjoy its blue fire at least once.

It soon became obvious that very few of David's friends
were going to be kept away by the falling snow. In no time
they had filled the drawing room and were spilling over into

the hall and dining room, and a beaming Mrs. Rogers assured Diana that it was "just like old times."

Diana had never seen David entertain in his own home, but she might have known he would do it with style. He had the good host's happy knack of enjoying his own party, and everything was going splendidly. Toward the end of the afternoon Vinnie appeared with her boyfriend and two of her brothers, and shortly afterward Gian-Carlo arrived with his pretty wife. Everyone seemed to like everyone else, and it was a sociable, good-natured crowd.

It's a good party, Diana was thinking happily, when suddenly it stopped being good. She heard a slightly tipsy laugh, and Marcia Beresford swept in with several young men.

"Sorry, David," Diana heard one of them say quietly. "I did my best to steer her somewhere else, but you know Marcia when she's had a few drinks. We won't stay long. We're expected at another party."

"Don't let it worry you," David answered calmly. "It's not important anymore."

Diana saw Vinnie swing around. "Oh, Lord! That's torn it. That woman says absolutely anything and everything that comes into her head. I'll go and see if I can distract her."

Well, if anyone can, it will be Vinnie, Diana thought, not too disturbed. Then, with an awful jar, almost like the thud of a physical blow, she remembered the photo, remembered the sweet face of the little boy looking down on that sophisticated company from the place of honor. Suddenly she knew with an awful foreboding that she must remove it. She dashed to the drawing room, but she was already too late. Marcia was stepping toward the mantelpiece and looking up.

"What a dear, sweet picture," she gushed. "Isn't he a darling?" She raised both hands to pick up the photograph.

"Put that down!" David's low, threatening voice startled the nearby guests into silence, and through it Marcia's voice rang clearly.

"No need to bark at me, David. John Barrington mentioned the other day that he had photographed Kris's baby. And hasn't he done a splendid job? Those brown eyes are just Kris all over. How clever of Barrington to catch the resemblance so strongly.

"I must say I was surprised when Barrington told me that you had the baby tucked away here," Marcia went on, "but then—" her green eyes inspected Diana mockingly "—he didn't mention that you had taken on the, er, nursemaid as well. Clever you." She patted David's cheek. "Now do forgive me for dashing off, won't you? I just dropped in to wish you a merry Christmas." She smiled winningly and swept out as swiftly as she had come.

Vinnie was by Diana's side in an instant. "Keep your chin up," she whispered. "Everyone can see that she's slightly tight, but none of them know what she's talking about. I'm sure Marcia herself doesn't know what she has done. Think about it. Nobody—but nobody—knows the situation between you and David."

"Yes, but David—"

"Look, everyone will be gone soon, and you can talk to him then. You were going to do it tomorrow, anyway. Remember your deadline. Nothing has changed except that he has been tossed in at the deep end."

Diana looked around for David. He was carrying on as host with cold efficiency, his face a mask. She could stand no more. She turned and ran upstairs.

For a while she sat on her bed in the dark until the nausea caused by nervous shock had left her. She had known that this night would come, but she had hoped to control the timing herself, to explain to David her false position, reaching for words that would give him the least pain...the most understanding. But now...now she didn't know what to do, where to begin. The sounds from downstairs had stopped some time ago. She knew she must go down at once and try to repair the damage that had been done.

As she entered the drawing room David rose to his feet, and she searched his face for a little compassion, but he looked at her as if she were a total stranger. "David," she ventured, "Can we talk?"

"You can, I hope. You must surely have plenty to say."

It was going to be more difficult than Diana had expected. She had known the truth would shake him, but in the back of her mind there had lingered the hope that when the initial shock was over, perhaps he would be happy to know that she had not, after all, been his brother's mistress.

Diana moistened her lips and started again, "David, when Jeremy—"

"Stop!" he hissed. "Leave my brother out of this. How dare you mention his name?"

She looked at him, thunderstruck. How could she even begin her explanation with such a restriction? Jeremy was at the heart of the whole matter. "Oh, David, please. Let me tell this my way," she begged.

"Let me help you." His voice was glacial. "Start, for example, with why you foisted a stranger's child on me."

Diana stared at him, astounded. Certainly Kris had been a stranger to him, but no more than she herself had been when they had first met. "Oh, David," she cried, "I know I should have told you about Kris...that I shouldn't have misled you, but I was afraid for Noel, and—"

"'Misled'!" The contempt in his voice ripped at her. "My God!"

Then she saw the sag in his broad shoulders, and her heart went out to him, and she tried again. "I know this has hurt you. I know I should have told you a lot sooner, but in a little while you'll see it's not...not that important." Had he really forgotten that Noel was still his brother's son?

He swung around. "Not important?" His eyes blazed into hers. "God in heaven! I wanted you. Have you forgotten so soon? I loved my—my brother's lover! There were nights that I sweated blood over the thought that you and he—that you had made a baby together. But I loved my brother, and I came to terms with what I thought was the truth. But this Kris, whom everyone seems to know except me. Don't expect me to take that in my stride."

Diana shook her head to try to clear it. She was completely bewildered. If that was truly how he had felt about herself and Jeremy, why was he still so distressed? After all, Noel was still David's nephew, nothing could change that, and he had said he loved both Jeremy and herself. Surely what he had just learned should be welcome information. In fact, surely her sister, whom David had never known, was only a minor character in this tragedy. And yet David seemed obsessed with her. Kris, Kris, Kris! Why did he bring up her name over and over? She couldn't grasp it, and she was too upset at that moment to think things through. She would go back to it later for she knew she wasn't thinking straight at the moment.

Diana felt she had been knocked off balance, not only by the violence of David's reaction, but by the extraordinary turn it had taken. She had expected recriminations—of course she had—and she knew she deserved them, but David's wrath against Kris was quite uncalled for. She had carried Jeremy's child with deepest love, and Diana had hoped that she could tell David Farnham about this very devotion that had cost Kris her life. She had wanted to assure him that his brother's son had had a wonderful mother, but there seemed little chance that he would listen to her now.

She had rehearsed many times, over and over, what she might say and what David might answer, but nothing had prepared her for this. "Oh, David, please...please..." she tried once more. "It's all my fault. I should have—"

"I see," he broke in savagely. "I suppose this Kris who left you with a baby to bring up has nothing to answer for? Nothing to be blamed for?"

"But Kris died a year ago," she said, her mind in chaos.

For a moment he stood unmoving, and then a cynical smile crossed his lips. "That's the last irony. A living enemy is bad enough, but a dead one..." He stormed out of the room, and a minute later she heard the front door slam.

Diana fled to her room, and for long, tortured hours questions twisted and turned in her mind until she was exhausted with trying to find answers. Was it she who had done this to David, or had her love for him blinded her to the real man? Had the autocratic arrogance that had sometimes bothered her early in their acquaintance been the true David Farnham after all? She didn't know. She knew only that she would have to get out of his life.

The man she thought she loved had never really existed.

VINNIE TELEPHONED her first thing the next morning and came over immediately when she heard the misery in Diana's voice. "Cheer up, my love. It can't be as bad as that," she said as soon as she entered the room.

"Believe me, it is," Diana told her. "Some of the things David said last night were simply incredible."

Vinnie was startled. "Tell me."

Diana told her word for word and Vinnie stared at her, aghast. "It's wild!" she exclaimed. "If you hadn't told me yourself, I never would have believed it. For David Farnham to talk to any woman like that is absurd, but to *you* it's...it's... Words fail me. I would have sworn that he was head over heels in love with you."

Diana sighed. "In any case it's all over now. Somehow I'll have to pick up the pieces. I'll...I'll...manage somehow."

"Of course you will. Keep your nerve. There must be an explanation somewhere," Vinnie said. "And to give Marcia credit, although it goes against the grain, I don't think she knew all she was stirring up. There is no way she could have known that David didn't know the truth about the baby. She just dropped in to be a cuckoo in what she suspected was a love nest. And I honestly think you should give David a bit more time. He's had a big shock, any way you look at it."

"You didn't hear him," Diana said. "But anyhow I can't walk out on the baby. I must stay until David cools down to be sure that Noel will be properly looked after."

"Of course you must," Vinnie agreed. "Just don't rush things."

"I don't think all the time in the world will do a bit of good," Diana said sadly.

After Vinnie had left, Diana heard a knock at the door of her apartment and opened it to David.

She scanned his face for some encouraging sign, no matter how slight, but she could find none. And rather than sitting down with her, he stayed standing.

"There isn't much for us to talk about," he said bluntly, "but what there is, is important and needs to be discussed now. I'm leaving tomorrow to do the same tour that took my brother so conveniently out of the country before Noel was born. I've decided to go myself this time instead of sending a deputy."

What on earth did he mean by "conveniently"? she wondered. Jeremy's leaving had been devastating.

"This will give you time to make arrangements for yourself and the baby," David went on.

"The baby?" Diana gasped.

"Of course. Surely you don't expect me to keep him now. He's your responsibility, and yours alone—at least until some other gullible man comes along."

Diana felt the blood drain from her face at the insult. It was all she could do to keep from crying out. She'd thought that David loved Noel. But, then, she'd almost believed that David loved her, too. How could she have been so mistaken? How?

"You may remain here for another few months until you hear from my office. They will give you plenty of notice as to when I'll be back, and I shall expect you to be gone by that time. No doubt that will be suitable."

Suitable for what? Diana wanted to ask as her temper rose to her rescue. She was too numb to feel much hurt for herself, but for David to toss the baby aside like a rag doll was inexcusable. The little boy had done nothing more than love him. The memory of them together brought tears to her eyes as David walked out of the room.

She had expected some discussion about Noel's future, and she had made up her mind to agree to almost any terms, for she'd felt that David would want what was best for Noel . . . as she did. But how was she to cope with this—this nothingness?

It was a question she asked Vinnie when her friend, still worried about her, came back that afternoon.

Vinnie could offer little comfort. "You know, if you were talking about anyone but David Farnham," she said, shaking her head, "I would say the man had gone off his rocker. He's still the baby's blood uncle any way you look at it."

"I know..." Diana agreed. "I always thought the great bond between them was that Noel was Jeremy's son. He seems to have forgotten that. I expected him to be disappointed in me, but to take it out on the baby..." Again tears choked Diana.

"Still, maybe when he gets over the first shock, he will see things differently," Vinnie repeated halfheartedly.

"Oh, no. He wants me to go and to take Noel with me."

"He what—?" Vinnie stared at Diana openmouthed. "That does it! The man needs a doctor. You know," she went on, "it's possible that the wreck of his first marriage was harder on him than people suspected. The way he's acting now is just too unreasonable."

"Well, I must find somewhere else to live right away," Diana said. "There is no way I can stay on here."

"Now be sensible. Take some time to mull over the situation. It won't be easy to find the right place, and David will be away for months. Nobody is waiting to move in. Take your time. And, who knows, he might still come to his senses."

"Never!" Diana exclaimed. Vinnie might be hopeful, but she knew better.

Moreover, how could she explain, even to her best friend, that in this house the thought of the "real" David would come too often in the night, come to stir again the hunger for his arms, for the sweetness of his mouth, for the warmth of his body? No, she must shut David out of her life, and she must do it quickly.

If only it were as simple as shutting the door to his house.

CHAPTER TWELVE

SEVERAL NIGHTS LATER Diana was startled when her telephone rang a few minutes after midnight. She was even more startled when she heard the voice on the other end of the line.

"Diana—" David's words came through a poor connection as if from the other end of the world. "I have just had a cable from my father forwarded to me from the office. He believes I am still at home, and he and my mother are on their way to London. I tried to reach them, but they had left the ship."

"I see," Diana said. "So I suppose you want us to get out of your house before they arrive."

"No—that's the last thing I want." She heard the edge of impatience in his voice, and she could sense the effort he was making to control his temper as he spoke with measured care. "Don't you understand? They are coming home to see their grandson." The bitter laugh that followed made Diana cringe. "I hadn't expected them for several months yet, and I've had no time to make any explanations."

That didn't surprise Diana. David didn't seem able to explain things to her, far less to his parents. "Surely there is nothing I can do for you...."

For a moment he was silent, then the words seemed to explode from the receiver. "How can you be so heartless?"

"Shouldn't I be asking you that?" She felt bewilderment mix with her anger.

Again he was silent for a moment. "Do you really want me to kill my mother!" he asked finally. "In her weakened condition, another shock could do just that. To hear that she had a grandson must have been shattering, and now to lose him..."

"Why blame me?" Diana asked. "It's you who's keeping the baby from her now."

"Are you trying to blackmail me?" he asked angrily.

Diana gasped. "How dare you say such a thing!"

There was a strained silence and then he spoke again, this time more calmly. "Diana, please let them think that things are just what they expect them to be until I get there...until I can find the least painful way to explain."

She could feel the effort he was making to plead with her. She knew, or thought she knew, how much he loved his parents, even though she now felt she shouldn't be sure of anything about David. But her heart went out to the woman who had already lost a son. Did she have to lose a grandson too? It simply didn't make sense that David Farnham could allow his pride to stand in the way of his mother's happiness.

"Very well," she sighed, "I will tell Mrs. Rogers to expect them. And I give you my word, if you think you can trust it, that I will do nothing to upset your mother. I'll leave that to you," she couldn't help adding bitterly.

She heard his quick intake of air, and he hung up with a cold "Thank you."

DAVID'S SECRETARY PHONED the next day to say that Sir Edwin and Lady Farnham would be arriving that evening but that David's flight had been held up by bad weather. "They'll be so pleased with the baby, madam," Mrs. Rogers said when Rogers was leaving to pick up the Farnhams at the air terminal, and Diana could see that she and Ro-

gers were delighted at the thought of seeing the elder Farnhams again. "I just wish Mr. David could be here when they
first meet the little one. It will be a day to remember."

It will indeed, thought Diana, and her heart failed her.
She had no idea what to expect from David now. If only he
hadn't told his father about Noel in the first place. Then she
remembered with a pang of sadness how happy David had
been for his parents' sake. There was no way she could have
refused to let him pass the news on. It was too late now to
keep Noel entirely from his grandparents, and if David insisted on making this break between himself and the baby,
it would make another tragic rift in the family.

To some extent Diana blamed herself. If David's behavior was extraordinary now, who could really blame him? He
had every right to feel resentment at having been deceived
for so long. She wished only that he wouldn't take that resentment out on Noel. Perhaps it was just as well that David had been delayed. For a few hours she would have only
his parents to cope with.

Hoping for the best she went upstairs to get ready for the
visitors. She put on a simple blue dress that did nice things
for her figure and enhanced her coloring. Then she brushed
her hair into face-framing waves and applied discreet make-
up with careful fingers. She was just finishing when she
heard the car return.

As David's parents came into the hall, Diana was glad she
had taken some trouble with her appearance. At first they
looked at her with a sort of kindly anxiety, and then they
both smiled at her in obvious approval. She could see that
Lady Farnham had been ill. There was a too-slender look
about her, but she held herself with dignity, and Diana felt
David's mother would have to be very tired indeed before
her slender shoulders would bow. Sir Edwin was all Diana

had expected. An older but equally handsome edition of his tall son.

Mrs. Rogers, who had been hovering in the background, was affectionately greeted by them both. The housekeeper took their coats, and Diana accompanied them to the drawing room.

"May I pour you something to warm you?" she asked, motioning to the drinks table.

Lady Farnham smiled. "My dear, it's kind of you, but I can't wait another minute to see my grandson."

Diana nodded. She had warned Polly about the grandparents' arrival. "Of course," Diana said, "but surely you are much more at home in the nursery here than I am. Why don't you just go up by yourselves and meet him?"

They quickly left the room, and Diana saw Sir Edwin's arm go around his wife, comforting and loving, as they turned toward the stairs.

It was some time before they came down again. When they did, Diana could see that they had been deeply moved by meeting the little boy, and she was touched by the mixture of joy and sadness on their faces. She knew she had been right in letting them go up to the nursery alone. They were the sort of people who would hate to make a show of their emotions, and Diana would have felt like an intruder watching them meet their late son's child for the first time.

Lady Farnham said, "He is absolutely beautiful." Then she turned to Diana. "Thank you, my dear," she said, and Diana knew that her gesture in staying downstairs had been understood.

Then Lady Farnham asked if she could have a light meal served in their suite. Diana could see that she was worn-out and that Sir Edwin was concerned about her. She poured them a sherry and then left them to sit quietly by the fire while she arranged things with Mrs. Rogers.

"Best thing for them," agreed the housekeeper. "Give me about twenty minutes, madam, and I'll turn down her ladyship's bed and set up a nice little buffet for their dinner. Sir Edwin can serve," she laughed. "It won't be the first time."

When Diana went back to the drawing room, Sir Edwin and Lady Farnham were contentedly sipping their sherry and looking up at Noel's picture on the mantelpiece.

"He is perfect, my dear," Lady Farnham said. "Everything we could have hoped for. It has made this New Year happier than I would have thought possible. We are so grateful to you."

"Yes, quite...quite," Sir Edwin agreed, and then was blowing his nose with unnecessary vigor.

Diana sighed when they went upstairs. They were such lovely people. She resolved to clear up this intolerable situation with David as quickly as she could. He had simply no right to put any sort of barrier between Noel and such wonderful grandparents. She hoped, too, that they would be able to change their son's mind. Only about Noel, of course. David's feeling for her need not concern them.

She sat by the fire for a long time in case there should be some word from David, but toward midnight she went up to bed. She was on the point of switching off the light when the telephone rang. It was David, to say that he was at the airport.

"Don't rout out Rogers," he said. "I'll get a taxi from here. Have my father and mother arrived?"

"Yes, but they went to bed some time ago."

"Then don't disturb them. Tomorrow will be soon enough." There was a pause and then he asked, "Have they seen the baby?"

"Yes." She hung up quickly and turned away from the telephone. She had endured an anxious and trying evening, and she was thoroughly tired of the whole hurtful situation.

Sometime during the night of restless tossing and turning she made up her mind that it was the last one she was going to spend in this awkward situation. With that in mind she marched down to the breakfast room next morning, determined to see David before the others came down.

She thrust the door open and glared at him for a moment, then told him forcibly, "David, whatever explaining you intend to do, do it soon. I heartily dislike being in a false position where your parents are concerned."

He looked at her icily. "Aren't you the last person in the world to criticize me for any deception regarding Noel? Surely your own deception went on long enough, starting with Jeremy and continuing with me."

Diana looked at him, astounded. She shook her head, trying to understand what he was talking about. Nothing he said seemed to make sense to her these days. "David, please," she cried, "I just don't know what you're getting at."

"Don't you? My dear girl, you're either very naive—or you think I am. Did you really expect my brother to go on keeping this baby?"

"Well, of course I did. He had already taken on that responsibility."

"Well, it must be a great disappointment to you to find that this Farnham refuses to be such an easy mark."

Diana watched fury struggle with contempt on David's face and felt her own anger flare, but they both held their feelings in check as Lady Farnham walked into the room.

She looked at them quietly for a moment and then said, "David, what a lovely surprise. When did you get back?"

"Late last night, too late to wake you," he said and bent to kiss her.

His father came in then and slapped David heartily on the back. "Your mother and I are delighted with the boy...and with Diana, too, for that matter." He beamed at Diana. "We've just come from the nursery, and I like that Polly. Nice, sensible woman."

"He's only saying that because Polly invited him to come and see Noel having his bath," Lady Farnham said with a laugh.

"Mother, you're looking so much better," David said. "The trip has certainly been good for you."

"Actually, it's seeing her grandson that's put her back on her feet, but then that young man would be a tonic for anyone." Sir Edwin smiled fondly at his wife, and Diana saw David wince and then recover his composure as he held a chair for his mother.

"Come and have breakfast and you can tell us all about your wonderful cruise," he said with forced cheerfulness, motioning Diana to join them.

There was a great deal to talk about, and fortunately Sir Edwin seemed quite unaware of any constraint; but Diana wasn't sure about Lady Farnham. Had she already sensed that something was very wrong between David and herself?

"Will you excuse me for an hour or so?" David said after some time, getting to his feet. "I must explain to the office my sudden return and tell them where I can be reached." He strode out of the room quickly, followed shortly by his father who mumbled something about being needed in the nursery.

Diana was now alone with Lady Farnham, and she still wondered how much of David's angry outburst had been overheard by his mother. "I'm sorry that—that you found David and me on the outs this—this morning," she faltered.

"Don't worry about me, dear. I know the Farnham men are not the easiest in the world to understand, but they *are* worth the effort and, in spite of what you may have thought at one time in your life, they are the soul of honor."

Diana felt the beginnings of a sob shake her. Until a short time ago she would have agreed with Lady Farnham, but now she wasn't so sure.

Lady Farnham seemed to sense Diana's distress for she said, "You sound as if all the cares in the world are weighing you down."

A lump rose in Diana's throat at the sympathy in Lady Farnham's voice, and she wondered if she dared confide what deep trouble she was in. It would be such a relief to tell someone who really knew David just what had happened. Suddenly she decided to jump in with both feet. After all, what did she have to lose and maybe—just maybe—Lady Farnham might be able to throw some light on David's strange behavior.

"I'm afraid I haven't lived up to David's expectations..." she ventured tentatively.

Lady Farnham gave her a puzzled look. "He must have been expecting rather a lot, then," she said slowly but with a comforting smile.

"No, no. I deceived him badly—and quite intentionally," Diana insisted. "I though it out very carefully beforehand, but there was a great deal more involved than I realized. Believe me, to hurt David was the furthest thing from my mind. How could I possibly guess that it would change his feelings for the baby?"

When she saw Lady Farnham start at the mention of Noel, Diana wished she hadn't said the last few words. She must keep cool, she warned herself, and tell her side of the story, but as objectively as she could. Above all she must be careful not to mention David's rejection of the baby. That

must be purely his business now, something that he alone
must sort out. David had made it quite clear that as far as
he was concerned the baby was now Diana's responsibility,
but she knew that if he wanted to, he could take Noel away
from her with the greatest of ease. She had never felt so torn
apart in her life as she did at that moment, weighing her own
possessive love for Noel against all the things his grandparents could do for him. Now that she had met them, she was
absolutely sure that they would never turn their backs on
Noel...and why David should want to turn his was the
biggest mystery in this whole affair. Lady Farnham's voice
brought her back to the present.

"You are making rather terrible charges against yourself, Diana."

"Yes, they are terrible, and for a time I thought I could
make reasonable excuses for them, but David is not the kind
of man who will accept excuses easily."

"Perhaps not, but he would never be unfair," Lady
Farnham insisted and then continued. "If you want to tell
me more, Diana, I shall try to listen with an open mind.
David doesn't often make mistakes but I know that when he
does, they tend to be like himself—a bit larger than life."

Diana knew she was being offered sympathy and understanding and suddenly she was almost sure that if she were
to tell Lady Farnham the whole story, the older woman
might be able to explain her son's extraordinary change of
heart. In any case it was worth a try.

"It's about Noel," she began as Lady Farnham sat very
still, paying rapt attention. "You see, he is not my child...he
was my sister's." Diana heard her listener's quick intake of
breath, and went on. "Kris died a few hours after Noel was
born, and I promised her that I would take the baby as my
own. When David turned up I was afraid that he would take
Noel away from me and..." Diana continued with the story,

telling every detail clearly and making no attempt to white-wash her own deception.

When she had finished, Lady Farnham sat motionless, saying nothing. Then she shook her head as if to clear it, and finally, after a long silence she looked at Diana with evident compassion. "My dear, you've had a dreadful year," she said, "and you did a great deal for that little boy with no help from anyone. Many a girl in your position would have dodged the responsibility. Surely David can see that."

"I don't know what he sees or thinks these days," Diana sighed.

"I must admit that I am as mystified by his behavior as you are," Lady Farnham said. "I can't for the life of me understand his antagonism. He is usually the most magnanimous of men. How can he be so angry with you when you have done so much for the newest Farnham?"

"I don't know. I just don't know!" Diana fought to hold back the sobs.

"Noel is the very image of Jeremy at the same age, except for the color of his eyes," Lady Farnham said, "although David wouldn't remember. He was too young when Jeremy was born to recall much of what his new brother looked like, but surely Mrs. Rogers noticed the strong resemblance. Didn't she mention it?"

"I don't think so," Diana said. She remembered that Mrs. Rogers had merely decided that Noel was completely and utterly wonderful, and that was that.

"This extraordinary attitude of David's is beyond me," his mother went on. "It seems completely out of character. David loved his brother and as far as I can see you did everything you could to save Jeremy pain."

"It was my fault for putting off telling David about my sister for so long," Diana admitted. "I just wanted this Christmas to be happy. I had made up my mind to tell him

everything right after the holidays. *Truly* I had." A sob
shook her.

Lady Farnham looked at her intently. "I see," she said.
"Noel isn't the whole problem, is he?" Her calm eyes
questioned Diana. "Obviously you are as much in love with
David as he is with you."

"What!" Diana shook her head. "No, you are quite
wrong. David loathes me."

"Oh, no, my dear," Lady Farnham protested. "You forget, I have known David intimately for thirty-two years. I'm
not likely to make that sort of mistake about him. But still,
his present behavior is quite bewildering. He is making a
mistake somewhere. Believe me, my splendid David is in
love—and for the first time, too."

Diana gasped. "The first time?"

"Oh, yes. Infatuations don't count, and he's no fool. He
wouldn't make a serious mistake about a love twice." His
mother nodded confidently.

Diana felt tears rising. "I admit there was a short time
when—when I thought he loved me, but . . ."

Sir Edwin's return from the nursery stopped the conversation. "Good to have a baby in the family again, isn't it?"
he asked happily, walking into the room.

Diana's tears were about to spill over and when she knew
she could not hold them back, she fled to her apartment.
Once there, she paced her sitting room restlessly. Lady
Farnham had been wrong about David's feelings, but her
sympathy had been warm and comforting, and had helped
a little.

The elder Farnhams were going out to lunch, and soon
Diana heard them leave. As the front door closed behind
them, she suddenly felt alone and bereft, but only for a short
while. Then anger began to shake her. What right had David Farnham to turn her life upside down? He had no

right—no right in the world—to treat her as he had. She resolved then and there to put an end to his bullying, and to
have it out with him the moment he got home. She resolved
to set her own world to rights again, and after that there
would be only one thing to say to David Farnham.

Stay out of my life!

CHAPTER THIRTEEN

DIANA'S ANGER smoldered steadily as her frustrated footsteps crossed and recrossed the room. Her anger was at flashpoint by the time she heard David return. She drew a determined breath, walked firmly down to his study and rapped on his door. She waited for no reply but walked straight in.

He leapt to his feet. "No one—" he glared at her "—no one comes in here uninvited!"

Diana glared right back. "That may be, but I have things to say, and I intend to say them here and now. I am sick and tired of waiting for your precious 'explanations' to your parents, tired of your sneers and insults. I have just been talking to your mother—not to help you, I assure you, but to save her some pain. God knows what you intend to tell her, but I have seen to it that she knows the truth. I have told her all about how I deceived you, all about Jeremy, all about Kris."

"You've what! Oh, God! My mother—I must go to her." He strode toward the door and would have pushed past her, but she reached it first and put her back against it. "Get out of my way!" he thundered.

"And let you go to your parents and fill them up with *your* version of Kris's wickedness. Darling Kris, whose only fault was to love your precious brother too well."

For long moments he stared at her, and Diana saw the crimson flush of anger ebb from his face. He stood as if carved in stone, and the anguish in his eyes as they burned into hers told her he was striving to work his way through deep confusion. Finally, in a hoarse whisper he said, "Diana, tell me about Kris."

She turned away from him. "Please, don't play any more games with me," she said bitterly. "You've known since the party that Kris was my sister, and that she was Noel's mother."

"Noel's mother! God in heaven! I thought this Kris was Noel's *father*."

Diana felt as if her breath had been knocked out of her. "Oh, no, that's intolerable! If you thought that, you must have believed that I . . . that I . . ." Words failed her, and she shook her head as if to clear it. "And where did you think Jeremy came in? Just another of my conquests?"

Her mind darted back to the party, to Marcia's "Kris's baby." And that was when Diana had fled in panic to her bedroom, and it had never occurred to her that nothing further had been said. But why should anyone have told David who Kris was? Those who knew—even Marcia—would simply have assumed that David also knew.

She looked at him standing before her, white and literally shaking. "How could you have believed anything so vile?" she asked. She remembered snatches of the wounding things he had said to her at the time: "You foisted a stranger's child on me. . . . Jeremy didn't deserve to be fooled," and many, many more. She had been too overwrought at the time to question them.

He looked at her helplessly. "Diana, I had no way of knowing the truth," he groaned.

"I tried to tell you the whole story that night after the party, but you wouldn't listen."

"I thought I knew the only part that was important to me."

"Important to *you*? I see! It was important that Noel wasn't your brother's son. His mother was of little consequence to you."

"No, you are wrong. She was of too much consequence."

"Too much? This is no time for riddles."

"I had come to terms with the fact that you had—had belonged to Jeremy, but the idea of you being with another man tore me apart. Some man named Kris. A dead man for whom you would lie so that your son—his son—would be cared for."

When the full magnitude of what he had believed sank in, Diana was heartsick beyond anything she had ever known. "Now I understand all those horrible things you said to me ... but how could you—?"

"A man—" he cleared this throat "—a man in love doesn't always think straight."

"Love! Do you call that love?" she demanded scornfully.

"No, it was jealousy. Tearing, raging jealousy over the man who had ... who had—"

"But the baby?"

"I never wanted to see him again, a living reminder that you had been in that other man's bed, and had deceived me...used me." Then, his voice was full of pain as he asked, "Diana, why? Why didn't you tell me from the start that you weren't Noel's mother?"

"I didn't know you. You were a stranger who had just walked into my life," she reminded him, "and I was afraid that you would take Noel from me. You had everything, and I had nothing to fight you with—no money, no friends, no influence."

"But surely you couldn't have believed that I would cut him out of your life completely."

"Why should I have thought anything else? To you he was the youngest Farnham. Nothing—not even his lovely mother—was of the slightest importance." When David made no answer, she turned and walked swiftly out of the room.

When she reached her apartment she sat down on the side of her bed, too dejected even to cry. How could David have thought all these dreadful things of her? How could she have been so mistaken about a man? But had she been mistaken? All that had happened was that he had made an error about a name, an error that had been blown up out of all proportion by her underlying deceit.

Then she remembered the despairing droop to his shoulders, how he had looked at her, saying nothing, only his eyes asking forgiveness. It was she who had done the hurting this time. And there was no satisfaction in that, not when she remembered the feel of his hard body, the warmth of his searching hands. Suddenly she was back in that wonderful night when he had held her so hungrily, and she had so eagerly answered his demands. She knew with absolute certainty that there was no way she could walk out of his life, no way at all.

In a panic she flew down the stairs and ran to his study. He wasn't there. She searched the rest of his rooms with increasing anxiety and then fled down the remaining flight of stairs to the drawing room. She breathed a sigh of relief when she saw his tall figure outlined against the firelight. He was standing as she had so often seen him, looking down into the flames. He lifted his head to look at her when she entered the room but he said nothing.

Well, what are you waiting for? she asked herself. She was a woman in love, and he was the man she wanted. Pray God he still did want her, she pleaded fervently as she walked across the room to stand beside him. "Please, David," she beseeched, her hand tentatively touching his sleeve, "please, would you just hold me?"

His arms, reaching for her, moved so fast that she was firmly held against his broad chest with her face buried against him before she had fully realized he had even heard her. She was crushed close to his racing heart, her tears dampening his shirtfront.

"Oh, darling, darling girl, please don't cry. I can't bear to see you miserable."

"I'm—I'm not miserable. I'm h-happy," Diana managed between sniffs.

"Good God, darling, if this is happy—" he smiled "—what do you do when you are sad?"

He loosened his hold a little so that he could look into her face. Then a gentle hand cupped her chin and raised her head to his. As his mouth came down on hers, first softly, and then with a famished intensity, her eyes closed, and she gave herself up to the sheer bliss of his kiss.

"My love, my dear love," he breathed, and as his scalding mouth probed her lips, she opened up gladly to this exciting foretaste of the virility his hard body promised. Then he cradled her as gently as he would a child against his chest. "Dear heart, will you ever be able to forgive me?"

"Shh. Promise you'll never say that word again," she said. "I made so many mistakes."

"We both did, my darling, but before I make any more, there is a question I want answered, and it's the most important question I will ask in my entire life."

Diana laughed happily. "The way I feel right now, you could ask me for anything . . . anything."

"Then, marry me."

"Yes. Oh, yes!"

Her body shivered against his with delight at the thought, and his mouth sought hers again in another long kiss. Then he pulled away with effort.

"Darling, I have to leave you for an hour." He smiled at her. "Can you live without me for that long? I have to arrange for someone to take my place on the Eastern tour. I can't possibly go now, can I?"

"Of course you can't," she smiled. "It would break my heart to have to do without you for all those months."

He gave her a quick kiss and made for the door. Then he dashed back for another, a swift, loving peck, and was off.

Diana drew a breath of sheer pleasure and sat down by the fireplace as she felt a beatific smile steal across her face. She didn't try to stop it, and was still sitting there in a state of euphoria when the elder Farnhams got back from lunch.

Lady Farnham gave her a long, inquiring look and then spoke with an inner satisfaction. "I see you've solved your difficulties. Good."

Sir Edwin eyed the two of them suspiciously. "What? Is something going on here I don't know about?"

"My dear, how could you possibly think such a thing," his wife asked, and then laughed as her husband looked at her keenly, and said "Humph!" and then disappeared behind his newspaper.

The three of them sat quietly for a while, and then Lady Farnham's eyes rested speculatively on Diana's flushed cheeks. "Diana, dear," she began, "what would you think of lending Noel to us for a few weeks? It would be good for him to get accustomed to coming to Glencarrick for his holidays, just as—just as the boys used to do."

Sir Edwin's paper fell suddenly, and Diana was touched by the hopeful look in his eyes. "That's a splendid idea," he agreed. "Do you think you could part with him for a while, Diana?"

Diana was startled, not so much at their request but at her own involuntary reaction. She loved Noel dearly, but the thought of being alone with David for the first time was temptingly sweet. "Are you sure he wouldn't be too much trouble?" she asked.

"Not if we had Polly, too," Lady Farnham said. "She knows Noel's routine, and there is a nursery in Glencarrick very like the one they are used to here. It's just as the boys left it. I—I never felt any need to change it."

"It would give us a chance to really get to know the little chap," Sir Edwin mused, "and it would do us all a world of good." Diana caught the surreptitious gesture he gave her indicating his wife, and she realized again that he was totally wrapped up in her welfare. Diana gave him a tiny nod in reply and was rewarded with a grateful smile.

"Of course you must have him, but do you mind if I just check it out with David first?"

"Let me do that, my dear," said Sir Edwin. "I have to make a call to the office, anyway, and I'll sound him out."

As soon as Sir Edwin had left the room, Diana turned quickly to his wife. "Have you told him about my difficulties with David?" she asked hurriedly.

"Yes, I have. Everything you told me, and he can't understand what's got into David, either. He called him a couple of rather rude names, I must admit," she said. "But he is sure there is a reasonable explanation somewhere."

"Oh, there is, there is," Diana assured her, and rapidly recounted her conversation with David. But only what Lady Farnham needed to know, for some of it was much too precious to be shared. She had barely finished when Sir Edwin returned.

"Well, that's settled," he announced as he went back to his chair. "David says we can have the boy next Friday."

Lady Farnham looked up from her needlework. "Friday? What has Friday to do with it?"

Diana was wondering that, too, and waited expectantly for the answer as Sir Edwin shook out the folds of his newspaper and donned his glasses, taking all the time in the world.

"Oh, apparently David's getting married that day," he said blandly.

"Wha-at?" Lady Farnham and Diana exclaimed at the same moment.

Sir Edwin looked at them over the top of his glasses, obviously delighted with the effect he had produced. "I had it from the horse's mouth," he added for good measure.

The two women looked at one another. "This is as much of a surprise to me as it is to you," Diana gasped.

"David was never one for wasting time," his mother said, "but if you want to get married, why not? Unless, of course, you would like all the trimmings, my dear. That could be managed quite quickly, you know."

"Oh, no, no!" Diana said. "All I really want is David."

When David came home Diana still felt slightly out of breath. "Father has told you the news, then?" he asked, his laughing eyes challenging the women.

Diana could think of nothing to say in front of his parents, but she felt a blush rise to her cheeks, and she knew real joy when she saw the unconcealed happiness written all over his face.

He went over and kissed her teasingly. "I'm sorry, darling. I couldn't manage it sooner. Even cutting red tape takes time."

"But, David," his mother said, "you are doing Diana out of her trousseau. It's not fair."

"Nonsense, Mother. We're honeymooning in Paris. Where better for a girl to buy all those incredible things she can't live without?"

"Where indeed?" Lady Farnham said. "I do wish I could be there to help you shop, Diana. There are—"

"No, Mother," David broke in decisively.

"Well," Lady Farnham said, sounding resigned, "at least I can give you my list of the nicest shops, Diana." She left the room taking her husband with her.

David dropped onto the sofa beside Diana, his arms reaching for her. When finally he came up for air he asked, "Am I really pushing you along too fast, my darling?" Then, as Diana shook her head, he went on, "You did say you'd marry me, remember? I just can't wait for you a moment longer than is absolutely necessary."

He kissed her again, and even Friday seemed a long way off.

CHAPTER FOURTEEN

As THEIR PLANE gently spiraled down toward Orly airport in Friday evening's twilight, Diana looked with delight at Paris spread below her like a delicate painting on watered silk. Jeweled lights drew her eyes along the great boulevards to L'Étoile, the fabulous star where the splendid streets met in the city's heart. Then the lights enchanted her by seeming to turn the bridges that spanned the darkly moving River Seine into diamond-encrusted clasps that held together its famed Left and Right Banks.

"How lovely!" Diana breathed.

"Just what I was thinking," David murmured, but when she turned to look at him he was showing no interest in the Eiffel Tower or the Champs-Élysées. Instead, his eyes were roaming gently from her lips, to her hair, to her eyes, to her neck, and back to her soft mouth again.

"Oh, David, you're not looking at the scenery," she protested with a smile. "How can you be so blasé about Paris?"

"My dear, tonight I can see nothing except my beautiful wife." He said no more, but his eyes continued to devour her, and the things they were telling her brought the warm blood to her cheeks.

A car was waiting for them at the air terminal, and soon they were in an elegant suite in the world-renowned Ritz Hotel.

Diana looked about the suite's sitting room with sheer delight. It was perfect. The antique French furniture, with its gentle colors and its ormolu trimmings, was as comfortable as it was beautiful, and the slightest movement of air brought a whisper of sound from the crystal lamps and a waft of perfume from great shallow bowls of gardenias and orange blossoms.

"Will it do?" David asked anxiously.

"Do?" Diana answered. "It's a fairy tale. I'm sure I'm dreaming."

"Go right ahead," David said and grinned, "as long as you remember that I'm the prince who kisses you awake."

His arms felt warm and safe around her, but even they couldn't quite ward off the tiny chill of...what? Was it trepidation that shivered up her spine?

If David noticed he made no comment. "Well, the suite has everything I need," he went on. "Cold champagne, a warm fire, a soft bed...and you."

He gave her a teasing smile, which she did her best to return, but the small shiver of anxiety was still there. It was obvious that he had ordered everything he could think of to please her. He hadn't needed to. She would have been happy anywhere as long as she was with him. But what if she disappointed him tonight? Perhaps there was something else she should have told him, so that he wouldn't be expecting more than she had to give. He couldn't possibly know how inexperienced she was.

He led her to the sofa and took a bottle of champagne from an ice bucket. The cork came out with a satisfying pop, and he poured the pale gold liquid into two delicate glasses. He handed her one and said, "Wait. The first toast is mine."

He stood before her, tall and straight and handsome and full of love and said, "To the most beautiful girl in the world—my wife."

Diana looked at him, and her heart turned over in loving delight. Dear God, she prayed silently, let me be everything he needs. Then she softly touched her glass to his. "To my darling husband," she said.

When she had emptied her glass, he took it from her and set it aside. Then he sat down beside her and gently picked up her hands. "And now, my love," he said calmly, "what is it you're afraid of?"

She should have known she would never be able to hide anything from him. She tried to smile, but it wasn't a success. "I—I'm a bit tired," she said, her voice quavering. "It's been an exciting day."

He leaned forward and placed a warm palm on either side of her face as he looked into her eyes. "Tell me," he commanded softly, and she tried to move her head aside but he wouldn't let her. "Tell me," he insisted, his voice quiet and sure. "Surely you know by now that I'll love you through anything."

"Please, David, I—I can't say this while I'm looking at you." She saw a little color leave his face and he dropped his hands to the sofa.

"Go on—" His voice was still gentle, but it held a note of authority that she recognized...and a note of worry as well.

"You see—" she tried to find the right words "—I, that is, how does...? Oh, dear, David!" Then it all came out in a rush. "I'm trying to tell you that I've never been to bed with a man before."

For a split second he gazed at her, thunderstruck. Then she heard a great gust of air escape him as he collapsed limp, beside her. Then he reached for her and lifted her bodily into his lap. "My darling girl, is *that* what's been worrying you? Is that what you were trying to tell me?"

His swift mouth stopped her reply, and for a long, long while he held her so close that she could have said no more even if she had wanted to. But there was no need. What he was telling her wordlessly with his lips and his hands made it perfectly clear that there was nothing to fear.

After a while she thought she heard a deep rumble in his chest ... and it came again. She sat up. "David, are you laughing?"

He threw his head back against the sofa and shook helplessly. "Yes, my darling."

"At *me*?" Diana gasped.

"No, sweetheart, just in sheer delight ... and relief. Thank heaven there is no history of heart attack in my family. As far as I can see, you are guaranteed to bring me to the brink of one about once a week. I thought you were carrying around some terrible secret that you couldn't bring yourself to tell me about."

"Well ... ?"

Suddenly his face sobered. "Oh, my dear love, can't you see what you've done for me? You are bringing me something that every man in this wide world would like to have ... a woman who is his, and only his."

"But—"

"Shh ... no buts. It's up to me to make you happy tonight." He smiled into her eyes. "Do you think I can?" he whispered. Then, when she hid her blushing face against him, he went on.

"I can wait no longer to find out, darling," he said, as he carried her to the bedroom and placed her on the bed.

He sat on the side of the bed and leaned over her to unfasten her dress. She helped his unaccustomed fingers with its intricacies, and very soon her last garment was gone at the tug of his impatient hands. She heard his quick intake of breath as he looked at her in the soft light reflected from the sitting room, and again she hid her face against him. He lingered for a second, holding her, and then rose to throw off his own clothes.

He stood before her for a moment, making no attempt to hide his need for her. She looked at him and knew that he was as much hers as she was his, and her breath caught in a sob of desire. In a moment he was beside her, gathering her nakedness to his own.

She gloried in the feel of his strength against her own softness, and she murmured his name as he brought his mouth down upon hers thirstily in a long kiss of deep desire. She loved the warmth of his hands on her breasts, felt herself arch involuntarily to offer them to him.

As he lifted himself over her, she felt within her a rhythm as old as time...the rhythm of his need for her, then she knew an earth-shattering desire that only he could satisfy, and she matched his compelling demand with her own insistence. His voice above her was deep and thick. "Oh, my sweet girl, love me—just love me." His great groan of rapture made her glory in her moment of pain as he carried her far over the edge of pleasure into unbelievable fulfillment.

Later she awoke from what seemed just a lovely dream, but when she felt the sweet roughness of his chest beneath her cheek, she knew it was real—and she was happier than she'd ever been in her life. When she turned her face to lay gentle lips against his chest, she felt his arms immediately tighten about her.

"Are you awake at last, sweetheart?" he murmured.

She made a sleepy reply and opened her eyes languorously. The tenderness of his smile melted her heart. She shifted herself to lean upon his chest and look down into his face. She traced his eyebrows, his nose, his lips, with a slender, loving finger. "David, you look positively smug," she said, and moved down to snuggle against his side again.

He gave her a broad grin. "I feel smug," he assured her. Then he propped himself up on an elbow and gazed down at her. He ran a warm finger along her cheek. "My darling, for a long time you have been a gorgeous girl. Now you are a most beautiful woman...my beautiful woman, and I can't tell you how glad that makes me."

"Maybe you can show me, my love," she murmured, and offered him her lips....

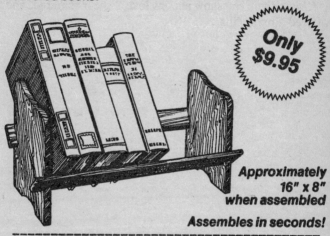

Can you keep a secret?

You can keep this one plus 4 free novels

MAIL-IN-OFFER
OFFER CERTIFICATE ✂

I have enclosed the required number of proofs of purchase from any specially marked "Gifts From The Heart" Harlequin romance book, plus cash register receipts and a check or money order payable to Harlequin Gifts From The Heart Offer, to cover postage and handling.

002

CHECK ONE	ITEM	# OF PROOFS OF PURCHASE	POSTAGE & HANDLING FEE
	01 Brass Picture Frame	2	$ 1.00
	02 Heart-Shaped Candle Holders with Candles	3	$ 1.00
	03 Heart-Shaped Keepsake Box	4	$ 1.00
	04 Gold-Plated Heart Pendant	5	$ 1.00
	05 Collectors' Doll Limited quantities available	12	$ 2.75

NAME _____

STREET ADDRESS _____ APT. # _____

CITY _____ STATE _____ ZIP _____

Mail this certificate, designated number of proofs of purchase (inside back page) and check or money order for postage and handling to:

Gifts From The Heart, P.O. Box 4814
Reidsville, N. Carolina 27322-4814

NOTE THIS IMPORTANT OFFER'S TERMS

Requests must be postmarked by May 31, 1988. Only proofs of purchase from specially marked "Gifts From The Heart" Harlequin books will be accepted. This certificate plus cash register receipts and a check or money order to cover postage and handling must accompany your request and may not be reproduced in any manner. Offer void where prohibited, taxed or restricted by law. LIMIT ONE REQUEST PER NAME, FAMILY, GROUP, ORGANIZATION OR ADDRESS. Please allow up to 8 weeks after receipt of order for shipment. Offer only good in the U.S.A. Hurry—Limited quantities of collectors' doll available. Collectors' dolls will be mailed to first 15,000 qualifying submitters. All other submitters will receive 12 free previously unpublished Harlequin books and a postage & handling refund.   OFFER-1RR

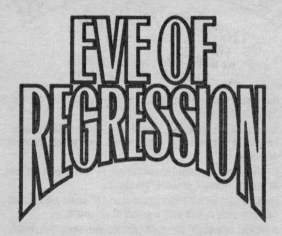

GIFTS FROM THE HEART
from *Harlequin*

FREE BY MAIL With proofs of purchase
plus postage and handling

A. **Hand-polished solid brass picture frame 1-5/8″ × 1-3/8″ with 2 proofs of purchase.**

B. **Individually handworked, pair of heart-shaped glass candle holders (2″ diameter), 6″ candles included, with 3 proofs of purchase.**

C. **Heart-shaped porcelain keepsake box (1″ high) with delicate flower motif with 4 proofs of purchase.**

D. **Radiant gold-plated heart pendant on 16″ chain with complimentary satin pouch with 5 proofs of purchase.**

E. **Beautiful collectors' doll with genuine porcelain face, hands and feet, and a charming heart appliqué on dress with 12 proofs of purchase. Limited quantities available. See offer terms.**

HERE IS HOW TO GET YOUR FREE GIFTS

Send us the required number of proofs of purchase (below) of specially marked "Gifts From The Heart" Harlequin books and cash register receipts with the Offer Certificate (available in the back pages) properly completed, plus a check or money order (do not send cash) payable to Harlequin Gifts From The Heart Offer. We'll RUSH you your specified gift. Hurry—Limited quantities of collectors' doll available. See offer terms.